THE CAMP WAS E

The fastest of them r... with a knife. Slocum fired and shot him through the lungs. The man fell, but more were coming up from behind.

Suddenly Slocum heard the girl scream. He leaped to his feet and sprinted back to the bedding, where a renegade was standing over her with a Bowie knife. Slocum shouted and the man turned just in time to see Slocum pull the trigger and fire. His head blew apart like a ripe watermelon, his brains spraying across the camp.

OTHER BOOKS BY JAKE LOGAN

RIDE, SLOCUM, RIDE
HANGING JUSTICE
SLOCUM AND THE WIDOW KATE
ACROSS THE RIO GRANDE
THE COMANCHE'S WOMAN
SLOCUM'S GOLD
BLOODY TRAIL TO TEXAS
NORTH TO DAKOTA
WHITE HELL
RIDE FOR REVENGE
OUTLAW BLOOD
MONTANA SHOWDOWN
SEE TEXAS AND DIE
IRON MUSTANG
SHOTGUNS FROM HELL
SLOCUM'S BLOOD
SLOCUM'S FIRE
SLOCUM'S REVENGE
SLOCUM'S HELL
SLOCUM'S GOLD
DEAD MAN'S HAND
FIGHTING VENGEANCE
ROUGHRIDER
SLOCUM'S RAGE
HELLFIRE
SLOCUM'S CODE

JAKE LOGAN

SLOCUM'S SLAUGHTER

PLAYBOY PAPERBACKS

SLOCUM'S SLAUGHTER

Published simultaneously in the United States and Canada by Playboy Paperbacks, New York, New York. Printed in the United States of America. Library of Congress Catalog Card Number: 80-80996.

ISBN: 0-872-16936-7

First printing August 1980.
Second printing April 1981.

Prologue

In semidarkness the old man stared at salt-encrusted stone blocks. He knew every line in them. Some he had made painfully with a scrap of nail, a scratch for each day. Nearly six years of scratches. He wasn't sure of the date, though. There had been the cholera epidemic, and the time when they took him from Dry Tortugas and shipped him to the mainland. There were the times when they put him in a better cell in the hope that good food and a dry place to sleep would make him betray the cause. He always tried to remember how many days he was away from the cell and, when inevitably they brought him back, to scratch them into the walls, but he wasn't sure he had them all.

The dungeon was silent. He smiled feebly at the thought. A dungeon. That was for medieval times, for backward monarchies, not for the Republic of the United States of America in the Year of Grace 1872 and of the independence of these United States the ninety-sixth.

But it was a dungeon nonetheless. They might call it a military prison and rename Dry Tortugas Key after the third president, but it made no difference. A dungeon was a dungeon. Idly he wondered, What would Thomas Jefferson have thought had he known they would name a dungeon Fort Jefferson?

Suddenly the silence was broken by tramping feet. A guard detail. He thought it was early for that. His knees ached from the rheumatism he'd caught—whether here or camping in the snow during the War of Southern Independence he wasn't sure, although certainly the salt damp of his cell hadn't helped—but despite the creaks and pops in his knees he got to his feet.

It was amusing to watch the guards. They huddled

together in a lockstep formation, each man's hand on the shoulder of the man in front of him, officers before and behind; Fort Jefferson was escape-proof, and bribing guards could do no good, because the guards were never supposed to be alone.

Sometimes, though: sometimes one managed to slip away from the others. Joseph Justice, formerly a slave. Formerly *my* slave, the old man thought. Joseph had enlisted and got himself posted to this horrible place, for no reason except to try to help his former master. A bottle of bourbon once in a while. A little extra food. And news from outside, news of Laura as she grew up on the frontier, news of Sandra and her husband, who mercifully had survived the war.

The guard detail tramped past, left-right-left-right, but then it halted.

"Prisoner, stand away from the door. Detail, left face. Port, arms! Sergeant, unlock the cell. Detail, stand ready to fire."

The old man laughed. All that, just to keep him from escaping! And they went through it every time they unlocked his cell door. Anyone's cell door. No one escaped from Dry Tortugas.

"And to what do I owe this pleasure?" he asked the officer.

"The prisoner will be silent."

"My rank, Lieutenant, is general. If this is a military prison, you are obliged by the laws and courtesies of war to use it when you address me. And you have not answered my question."

"Silence!"

"I do not choose to be silent."

The lieutenant seethed. He raised his swagger stick as if to strike. The old man stood fast, a half smile on his face. "Courage, Lieutenant," he said. "Surely you have enough to beat an old soldier. Even if you don't choose to face me on a field of honor."

The guard officer stepped back with a sour look. "Sergeant, position the prisoner into formation," he ordered.

"Yes, sir. General, by your leave, sir."

"Very well, Sergeant." The old man fell into the line.

Four privates closed up behind him. They marched through the stone corridors.

He heard stirring in the other cells. He could imagine the others peering out through the tiny barred windows in their cell doors. As he passed one cell, he waved silently to the man inside. The guard lieutenant almost said something, then caught himself. It was forbidden for anyone to speak to Dr. Samuel Mudd, the traitor who had set the broken leg of John Wilkes Booth; but the old general hadn't actually spoken to him, and besides, there wasn't really anything the lieutenant could do.

It was bright daylight when they marched up the steep stairway into the stone courtyard. The old man stumbled; his eyes were almost gone, unaccustomed to bright light. In the blazing Caribbean sunlight he seemed as pale as a worm, a thing almost ghostly.

"Where am I going?" he demanded.

This time the lieutenant ignored him. They marched across the courtyard and out the great gate to a small jetty. A sloop stood there. Or perhaps, he thought, not a sloop. He couldn't really tell. It was a small sailing ship, single-masted, only two cannon mounted; it flew the ensign of the U.S. Navy at the gaff of the fore-and-aft sail. A naval commander waited at the top of the gangway; marines stood on the jetty itself.

"Am I leaving Dry Tortugas, then?" he demanded.

The guard lieutenant still wouldn't answer, but the naval commander spoke down to him.

"Yes, General. We're taking you to Biloxi. It has been arranged for you to see Mr. Jefferson Davis."

That news brought him up short, so that one of the privates behind him almost ran him down. "President Davis?"

"The former president of the late Confederacy, yes, sir. Please come aboard, General. Lieutenant, we relieve you."

The old man walked wearily up the gangway. At its top he turned toward the U.S. flag, hesitated a moment, and finally brought his hand to his breast. Courtesy, he told himself. It means nothing. I am not acknowledging their bloody banner by saluting it.

They led him to a cabin and brought him a drink while the crew made ready to put the ship under sail. When he said he was tired, the navy officers left him alone, apologizing for the accommodations.

The tiny cabin was the greatest luxury he had enjoyed since the war.

Alone, he thought of what lay ahead. Would they really confront him with Davis? And what then? Would the president himself order him to give up his secret, the secret he had held for all these years?

And if Davis did order it, what then? Tell the Yankees?

Why not? The war was long ended. The Confederacy was dead. They told him little of the world outside his dungeon, but Corporal Justice brought him news when he could; of Reconstruction, of the South occupied, of poverty in Mississippi and Louisiana, poverty so grinding that few remembered that these were the two wealthiest states of the Union on the day the war began.

But the war was over. There had been amnesty for most; had Davis himself been pardoned? The last the general had heard, Davis was kept in irons in Fortress Monroe, his health failing while the Yankees tormented him but refused to try him, as they had refused to try the general himself.

His reverie was interrupted by a shout from the deck above. There were shouted orders, and he heard the rumble of the cannon being run out, then the unmistakable boom of a cannon fired from some distance away.

A voice carried clearly across the water. "Heave to, or we will sink you." The general started at old memories. Surely he knew that voice. He tried to remember, but it had been too long. There had been too many years in the damp basement of Dry Tortugas.

The deck heeled as the sloop came up into the wind.

I

The wind rose and blew dust across the rider. The summer of 1872 was hot and dry, and the high plains country south of Fort Dodge was covered with browned, straggly grass and the ever-present red dust. A few clumps of trees stood in patches along the dried-up creek beds, and the rider stayed as near to them as he could, seeking even a moment's relief in the shade before moving on westward.

His big bay gelding seemed accustomed to the heat and dust and made only a momentary protest whenever the rider passed without stopping at one of the tepid muddy pools dotting this tributary of the Cimarron River. The lone rider sat tall and straight in the saddle, and from a mile away it would have been clear to anyone that both horse and rider had spent time in the military.

Seen up close, the man didn't look so military. His clothes were cheap civilian stuff, not very old but already darkly stained with sweat and alkali. His saddle was the high-cantled Western ranch saddle, not the split McClellan favored by the U.S. Army. His hat was Mexican leather and looked as if a herd of buffalo had stampeded across it.

Although his clothes were not military, there were telltale signs of his recent past. He was clean-shaven. A pair of field glasses dangled from his saddle horn. Even after so many years he could still not get used to parting his hair on the wrong side to cover the faint red saber scar that ran from the edge of his hairline to the crown of his head. Sometimes he rubbed it without thinking.

His weapons were clean and well used: a cased Winchester .44 carbine in a saddle scabbard and a Colt Navy .36 on his belt. The pistol holster had once boasted a covering flap, but that had been cut away along with part of the leather so that it could be drawn more quickly.

From time to time his hand flew to the pistol and drew it with a smooth motion, thumb cocking the hammer, the weapon pointed at some rock or clump of sage grass. The military neither taught nor encouraged fast draws, and the rider was obviously teaching himself how to do it.

There was another pouch on his belt, with powder flask, caps, balls, two loaded cylinders for the revolver, and a bullet mold. His large sheath knife, of the design made popular by Colonel Bowie, was slung at an angle on his left side, easy to reach with either hand.

As he rode, he sent his eyes around the plains. He did not always turn his head, but the eyes moved constantly, alert to any possible danger. His watchfulness came from long habit, and he was hardly aware of it. Sometimes he stopped and used the field glasses to scan the horizon.

At high noon he sought a patch of shade in one of the small tree stands above a pool of muddy water. He dismounted and threw the saddle to the ground to serve as a pillow, then ground-tied his horse while he sneaked up on the relatively clear water at the top of the muddy hole. He eased his canteen gently into the water, skimmed the top scum away with his hand, and allowed the vessel slowly to fill from just below the surface. Only then did he let the horse approach the water hole, and even so he watched to see that this mount did not drink too much.

Slocum's gelding approached the water with the same reverence as its rider, betraying some genetic clue from the Arab side of its family. The horse drank daintily, doing its equine best not to roil the mud. Slocum sipped sparingly from his canteen and lay on the ground. At intervals he stood wearily to scan the horizon with field glasses again.

He saw nothing out of the ordinary. Ahead was a faint haze just at the horizon, a deep-purple patch that he knew was the beginning of the mountain range in New Mexico Territory that marked the western boundary of the Texas high plains. He spent a long time examining what might have been a wisp of smoke many miles ahead, but he saw nothing else and finally lay back down with his head on the saddle.

"Nobody following us," he told the horse. "Not likely anyone would be. Nobody gives a damn about us, not even Indians." The horse, whose name was Dorkus, nickered before bending his head to graze on the brown stubble. The animal seemed reassured by the man's voice. Like most cavalry mounts he wasn't used to being alone, and he didn't like it.

"Nope. Nobody around," John Slocum said. Then he laughed. "Not even the Indians care for this godforsaken place. Nor do I."

He gave the horse and himself a full hour's rest, then fixed and ate a cold lunch before topping up his canteen from the newly settled pool. When he had saddled Dorkus and mounted, he swept the horizon with his field glasses again.

The smoke ahead seemed thicker, and he frowned. Then he kicked the horse slightly to move him westward.

"My bloody word, it is hot," Slocum said. He grinned at himself. "You'd think after a hitch in the Yankee cavalry I'd swear like a trooper, not a Southern gentleman," he told the horse. Then, to prove he could do it, and because there wasn't anything else to do, he let loose a three-minute stream of obscenities and blasphemies without once repeating himself.

The horse seemed to like that and moved on with new life. Slocum laughed. Yankee mounts were not like the blooded horses he'd grown up with. The laugh faded out.

Nothing else was the same, either. His home was gone. When John Slocum rode back after Appomattox, he found his mother and sisters living with loyal blacks in the old slave quarters. Their home was occupied by a Pennsylvania carpetbagger family. His father had been killed by occupation forces. Whatever life he'd known before the War Between the States was ended, gone forever.

He'd never known any trade but the military. Virginia Military Academy, West Point, headed for the Regular Army of the United States; then came the war, and like a lot of Southern officers, he'd taken a commission with the Confederate States army. Shiloh, Chattanooga, Manassas, the Wilderness, the bloody hell of Cold Harbor; detached duty with Mosby's Rangers; he'd seen a lot of the war, and when it ended, he was a major of cavalry, an officer of a defeated and occupied nation.

At home he found the carpetbaggers. When he tried to get his land back, there had been a gunfight, and by dark the Yankee-appointed sheriff was searching for him. He couldn't go home again.

Like a lot of Confederate cavalrymen, he'd joined up for a hitch in the Yankee army, serving in the ranks because the Congress wouldn't allow Southerners to hold a commission. He'd gone to a frontier regiment and become a first sergeant and spent his hitch fighting the plains Indians.

It hadn't worked out. Sure, the colonel had called him the best trooper in the regiment, and Slocum could truthfully say that was close to right; but the U.S. Army after the war wasn't any outfit Slocum wanted to serve in, not as a ranker and not as an officer either. Slocum was too impatient. He fought to win—and the Congress and the president and the Indian Bureau and the hordes of speculators and sutlers and traders and drummers and politicians had got things so fouled up the army couldn't do its job.

Men in dirty blue uniform shirts rode out and died to consolidate a larger territory than the greatest empire of Europe, fighting the finest light cavalry in the world—Comanche and Kiowa—and the army had to fight with cast-off weapons and surplus from the war, with tired horses bought at outrageous prices, with inadequate supply and stupid officers. Sometimes the army fought without pay. The troopers died, though they generally won when they were allowed to. Slocum hated it all.

He'd finished his hitch and got out.

"And now what?" he asked the horse. "Our luck hasn't been so good lately." He frowned at the column of smoke ahead, then halted and took out the field glasses. "It's not running so good now, either," he said. "For somebody."

The smoke was closer now. It rose in a thin wisp into the dusty air, and now he could see the wheeling vultures above it. Slocum had seen those signs before and knew what they meant. He spurred the horse into a trot.

He rode cautiously, but he wasn't too worried. The buzzards were swooping low, and they never did that if there were people moving around below them. Fire and vultures: it could only mean one thing, and with the buzzards landing, nothing was likely to be alive. Even so he stopped frequently to scan the horizon with the glasses before riding on.

When he topped the slight rise and looked down on the ruins of the wagon, he was expecting what he saw, but still he had to swallow hard as he felt his lunch rising in his throat.

The charred remains of a man and a wagon wheel were still joined with a strip of wet rawhide. Fire had been built under his crotch, and he'd been slowly cooked to death. Another man lay nearby, dead of a dozen wounds. Both had been scalped.

When Slocum rode down into the dry creek bed where the wagon lay, he saw a naked woman lying still and twisted. From the ugly bruises and scratches on her hips and breasts and the blood between her legs, she'd been raped until she died.

Not far from the woman was a girl's dress. It was torn and filthy. Slocum looked at it and cursed. The dress was many sizes too small for the dead woman. It looked as if whoever had worn it wasn't a lot more than five feet tall, and certainly wasn't going to fat the way the dead woman was. Slocum stared at the dress and cursed again. Then he searched for more bodies.

He found none. From the blood splotches along the creek bed and out beyond it, the men had given a good account of themselves before they died; the raiders had to carry away a number of their own dead and dying. But he found no trace of the smaller girl.

Something thrashed in a clump of sagebrush twenty yards away, and Slocum sighed in relief. Let it be the little girl, he said to himself. Please. Let it be her.

It wasn't. It had been a man, but now it wasn't even that. Now it was a blinded, hamstrung creature that croaked from a throat whose tongue had been burned with a hot knife. It was a naked thing with the hair singed off, burned across the belly, flopping in the dust, screaming and beating its head against the dirt.

"Reckon I'd want to die, too," Slocum said, but he said it softly so that the man couldn't hear. Then he raised his voice. "I'm a friend," he called. "Hold on; I'll get the water."

Slocum swallowed hard, because he was going to need those cold beans he'd eaten at noon, and swung down from the saddle. He carried the canteen over and steadied the man's head, then splashed water into the ruined throat.

The man croaked something that might have been thanks, then screamed again. The blood was dried around his empty eye sockets, and they'd burned him to sear all his wounds so that he'd live longer. They'd like this joke, that the man had lived long enough for someone to find him before he died. They'd like that a lot. And they'd like the way the man's sightless face turned this way and that around the campsite like that of a hound seeking out a waning scent. They would giggle with delight at the way he would know his seeing days were over.

The man screamed again and again. "Laura!" he shouted. It was the only word he'd spoken that Slocum could understand. "Laura!"

"Your wife?" Slocum asked.

The man shook his head vigorously. "Laura!"

"Daughter?" Slocum asked.

The man hesitated, then nodded.

Jesus, Slocum thought. Jesus. "Is she full grown?"

Slocum cursed again when the man nodded. He looked at the smoldering wagon. It had been stripped, but here and there were enough fire-blackened goods to indicate that the wagon had been loaded for traveling. A cast-iron stove. And burned buffalo hides. From the tracks, it had been headed west.

What kind of damned fool would bring his family through here? This was miles below the "dead line," the line where army patrols stopped; it was well inside the area set aside for Comanche by the Medicine Lodge Treaty.

But the whites wouldn't stay on their side of it, and neither would the Comanche and Kiowa.

Most of the wooden parts of the wagon had burned away. Only the hides and quilts and a few thick blocks of wood smoldered, sending up the thin stream of smoke that had brought Slocum. There was horse sign, but the Indians had taken all the mounts. The oxen were just beginning to stink. They had not burst, save one, and only their eyes were gone.

Slocum assumed it was vultures until he saw how neatly the ox's belly had been opened. The beast had surrendered its liver to hungry savages while still struggling to breathe. He studied the eye sockets of the other animals and saw that somebody had anticipated the vultures. It was mystifying. He could understand bad feelings between people, but what had the oxen ever done to the Indians? This group must be some peculiarly brutalized lot of bleeders. He studied the signs. "Yesterday?"

The man croaked and nodded. Then he screamed something that Slocum couldn't understand, something about his general, Slocum thought, and finished by shouting "Laura!"

"She's not here," Slocum said. "Not dead, but not here."

The man shuddered. He turned his blind face toward the sound of Slocum's voice, and he crawled forward until he felt John Slocum's boots. His hands clawed upward, to the trousers, to Slocum's waist, and felt toward the pistol.

Slocum pushed him away. "In a minute," he said. "There are things I have to know. There was you, there's two more men dead, and—and a woman. She was killed clean," Slocum said, lying.

The man screamed. He knew. He had seen it, before

they burned out his eyes. Maybe they'd made him watch. They often did. He screamed again.

"Were there any more? Two men, a woman, and Laura. And you. Any others?"

"No. God! Laura!" He crawled toward Slocum again.

John Slocum backed away. "How many of them? More than twenty?"

"No," came the gasp.

"More than ten?"

A nod. The man crawled again, and again Slocum retreated. "More than ten, less than twenty. Rode off this morning, early. I guess that's all. You want to say any prayers?"

The man nodded. He stopped crawling and lifted himself to his knees. He raised his hands, and Slocum saw that the fingers of the left hand had been smashed and burned.

There was silence for a minute; then John Slocum drew the Colt and shot the man through the head.

II

"No shovel," Slocum muttered. Dorkus moved skittishly near the burned wagon. He nickered and blew at the smell of blood, then shied away. Even a cavalry horse can take only so much.

"Reckon I should do something," Slocum said. "But first—" He mounted and checked the horizon with the field glasses. "Bat puckey," he said. "There's somebody coming up from behind. Following us?" He lifted the glasses to stare again.

It was a lone man, dressed in a dark suit. The man rode confidently toward Slocum. "Now what's a dandy like that doing in Indian territory?" Slocum demanded. He rubbed the horse's neck. "Well, probably he's got no shovel either, but we may as well wait and see." Slocum rode up onto the top of the dry bed so that the approaching rider could see him clearly. Then, just for luck, he shifted the pistol in its holster, drew it, and spun the cylinder to check that none of the caps had fallen off. He reholstered the weapon and waited.

The newcomer came on at a trot. He didn't seem surprised to see Slocum, but when he reached the top of the creek bed and looked down at the carnage below, his face went green. He jumped from his horse and ran behind the trees. Strangled sounds came from over that way. Slocum waited until it was quiet again.

"Ho," he called.

"Ho." The newcomer came out wiping his mouth. He took his canteen from its place on the saddle and drank. The man was big, almost as big as John Slocum, and like John he had dark hair and eyes. His tan wasn't burned as deep a bronze, nor were his cheekbones as high, but from a distance the two men might have been related, cousins, or maybe even brothers.

The man's suit was a closely woven cloth. It reminded Slocum of the canvas suits some officers wore in the field, only theirs were generally a much lighter color. The man wore a wide-brimmed felt hat with high block, the kind that was popular in Texas. A polished leather belt circled his waist. Slocum couldn't see the pistol under the coat, but from the bulge he knew there was one. A new Henry repeating rifle was scabbarded on the left side of the newcomer's rig.

"Who the hell are you?" Slocum demanded.

"Jim Cavanaugh."

"Drummer?" Slocum asked.

"Right. Mine equipment." Cavanaugh kept his eyes on Slocum, carefully not looking down into the draw. "And you are?"

"Slocum. John Slocum. What brings you out to Indian territory?"

"Got a good chance to make a big sale in Sante Fe, if I can get there fast enough. Stage isn't running. Indians. Thought I'd strike west." He pointed down into the creek bed. "Looks like they tried it, too. You with them?"

"Nope. Riding west to Santa Fe, just like you," Slocum said. "Hell, you don't have a shovel." He swung down off Dorkus and walked down to the wagon, where he found a broken-off board that hadn't burned. "Want to help?" he called. He began scraping sand and dirt over the bodies.

"Sure." Cavanaugh came down. He almost heaved again when he saw the woman, but he managed to hold it down. He got another board and pushed sand and dirt over the corpses. "Won't do any good," he said.

"Nope. But we got to do it anyway."

Cavanaugh didn't say anything. Both men knew that the coyotes would have the dead uncovered by morning, but it didn't seem right to ride away leaving them unburied.

"We have a problem," Slocum said.

"How's that?"

"There was a girl in the family. Don't know how old, but full grown. Little girl, not much over five feet high. The Comanches took her."

Cavanaugh didn't say anything for a moment. He scooped more dirt over the woman, then went to the mud patch a few feet away and got fresh mud to throw on top of the dry sand mound. "Anything we could do?"

"Damned if I know," Slocum said. "There were maybe a dozen Comanche. Maybe a few more."

"You read sign that well?"

"Maybe. But I was told."

"Told? Were you here when—I mean, is there anyone alive from this party?"

"Not anymore."

"Oh." Cavanaugh shuddered. "I heard a shot."

"Yeah."

Cavanaugh looked thoughtfully at the hoof marks headed southwest from the creek bed. "A dozen or more of the bastards. Two of us." He looked up at Slocum. "Where do we go?"

Slocum pointed to the tracks. "That way, I guess."

"Looks like a good way. Shall we ride?"

"It's a fool's errand," Slocum said. "They're heading for New Mexico. This time of year there'll be trading with the Comancheros. Probably figure to sell the girl to the Comancheros."

"You seem to know a lot about them."

Slocum shrugged. "I rode with the cavalry awhile." They trotted on, hoofbeats sounding in the dusk. Neither of them had said anything about making camp. "Give a lot for a dozen men in dirty uniform shirts," Slocum said. "Blue or gray. Or Mexican soldiers for that matter." Or, he didn't add, a platoon of Maximilian's Légion étrangère. They'd been good men, as Slocum knew from his months as a mercenary in Maximilian's dying empire.

"Do you think they'll—what do you think will happen to the girl?" Cavanaugh asked. "If they intend to sell her, surely they won't harm her."

"You never know," Slocum said. "Nobody thinks like an Indian. Half the time they don't know themselves what they're going to do. Other times, they got a plan, but it's nothing you'd make sense of.

"Take these. Comanches don't usually gang-rape.

These did. This is a bad bunch, Mr. Cavanaugh. A bad bunch, and there must have been whiskey in that wagon for them to do what they did to the woman. Apaches, *they* rape; but Comanches are generally too proud."

They rode on for another mile before Slocum spoke again. "It's the buffalo hunters," he said. "There's supposed to be a peace. At Medicine Lodge the United States and the Comanche Nation called off the war. Set aside territory for the Comanche. But the buffalo hunters won't stay out. Make too much money. Two, three dollars a hide those hunters get, and that's a lot of money. Man can make a month's wages in a day hunting buffalo. But he has to take his chances on the Comanche. Don't blame the Indians much; the hunters kill off all the buffalo, the Comanche have nothing left to live on out here." He brooded for a few moments. "Still, they have no call to do that to women. And children. They don't do that to their own women and children, not in their wars."

Slocum reined in. "It's getting too dark to follow trail. Best we make camp now. Cold camp. Firelight'll be seen for miles out here."

Dawn came early on the plains. Cavanaugh and Slocum got out of their blankets, rolled them up, and lashed them behind their saddles. Neither man said anything. There was nothing to say. Each knew the other had spent the night wondering what was happening to Laura, a girl whose last name they might never find out.

When they were saddled up, they rode out on the trail, still not speaking. Cavanaugh passed several stale biscuits over to Slocum, who nodded thanks. The biscuits were better than the hardtack Slocum carried. He washed them down with water, wishing for time to make coffee for the morning.

An hour later they came to the end. The trail vanished in a myriad of tracks, thousands of tracks and a litter of fresh dung.

"The southern herd," Slocum said. "Buffalo. Wandered pretty far north this year."

"What do we do now?" Cavanaugh asked. He looked in dismay at the torn ground. "We'll never follow them."

Slocum sat in his saddle in silence for a moment. "Cavanaugh, I said this was a fool's errand to begin with," he said.

"True. Did we have any choice?"

"No. But I did some thinking last night. There were hides in that wagon, but nothing else a buffalo hunter would have. Don't seem to me those people would have killed and skinned that many themselves. I think they bought those hides from a hunting party."

"You figure the hunters are around here, then? I have to admit I don't know what the two of us will do if we catch up with the Comanches."

Slocum nodded. "Thought about that all morning. Decided if we found herd sign, I'd send you after help. Those hunters won't be far from the herd."

"If there are any hunters," Cavanaugh said.

"True. But there should be. Those hides came from somebody. And you're slowing me down, Cavanaugh. That horse of yours could beat mine in a mile race, but he can't keep up with Dorkus over the long trail. Seems to me you'd do best to see if you can find that hunter camp and bring help. Me, I'll try to stay behind this war party. I'll leave some trail sign along the way so it won't be hard to follow. That way you can all catch up to me."

"If I don't find help, you'll be in a bad way," Cavanaugh said.

"True enough."

"I don't like it. But I don't have any better idea. . . . Listen. Did you hear that? Sounded like a shot."

"Sure as hell was," Slocum said. "That was a Sharps Big Fifty, sure as hell. Buffalo gun. Maybe two, three miles away. That's buffalo hunters, all right. Go find them, Cavanaugh. I'll see if I can sort out the trail."

"Well—they're close enough. Why don't you come with me?"

"How'd you feel if that little bit of time was what killed the girl?" Slocum asked.

Cavanaugh nodded. "Bad. All right. See you later."

He wheeled his horse to the right and rode after the vanished buffalo herd.

Slocum rode on across the tracks made by the beasts. They had cut a swath half a mile wide across the dry grasslands. Slocum could remember when the herd was twice that large, maybe larger. Buffalo hunters had slaughtered hundreds of thousands, maybe millions. Slocum had once seen a thousand carcasses, stripped of their hides and left to rot on the prairie, and he had heard the Kiowa and Comanche chiefs rage at such waste.

He went across the buffalo tracks in a straight line, because he had an idea where the raiding party was heading. From the direction they'd been going, they were moving to the New Mexico boundary, just as Slocum had first suspected. This wasn't a full war party, John had decided. Probably a band of young Comanche looking for a chance to raid a neighboring clan for horses. The freight wagon just happened to be in their path. Bad luck for two men and a woman. Maybe worse luck for a little girl named Laura.

"Not such good luck for me, either," Slocum said to his horse. "A fool's errand indeed." But he rode on, looking for the trail, and was not surprised to see it start up again when he had crossed the swath made by the buffalo. He unrolled his blanket pack and took out his only spare shirt. After a moment's hesitation he tore strips from it and left one tangled in the grass so that it could be seen from a long way off.

Then he rode on, relentlessly tracking a dozen Indian warriors. There was a grim smile on his lips as he rode.

III

Slocum caught sight of the Comanche war band just before dusk. He had ridden hard through the day, and the stamina of his big cavalry horse had been severely tested. Indian ponies just couldn't keep up a pace like that.

By midafternoon he saw dust far ahead and was fairly certain it was made by the Comanches. The lords of the plains feared very little; certainly they were not afraid of the army, which didn't come into this territory —and, if it did, would come with clanking sabers and canteens and could be seen and heard for ten miles.

At dusk Slocum topped a slight rise and halted. He used the field glasses to scan ahead and saw them, a group of horsemen trotting in a tight bunch, too far away to make out details. They were framed against the setting sun, and it wasn't likely they would see Slocum behind them if he didn't get any closer. Come dawn, of course, the situation would be reversed, and he'd have to be more careful.

Once he had them spotted, he thought again just how bad his situation was. He was one, lone man against a dozen or more warriors, and however much he might hate them, he had to respect their fighting abilities. They called themselves "lords of the plains," and they'd earned the title. General Crook had called them the finest light cavalry the world had ever seen, and he hadn't been joking. The Indians were doomed. Buffalo hunters killed off their way of life with army encouragement. White men's industries and weapons would be irresistible in the long run, but just at the moment, the run didn't seem long at all.

Just at the moment, John Slocum was scared as hell. He said so to his mount, but then he laughed. He never considered riding on, leaving the trail and going on to Sante Fe as he had intended. Scared or not, he was the one representative of civilization. Of the United States, he thought with a wry smile. Although the United States wouldn't have been too proud of him.

But he was sure as hell going to teach those bastards a lesson if there was any way to do it. The Indians had some right on their side, and in their place Slocum would fight, too, but fight men, not make war on women and children.

Trouble was, he couldn't think of any lesson he could teach them.

Dark came fast on the plains. Slocum walked his horse carefully toward where he'd seen the Indians. When he'd come a mile, he staked Dorkus to a long tether, pushing the picket only halfway into the ground, so that if he didn't return, the horse could work loose and run away. He knew Dorkus wouldn't try that for hours, but eventually, if he got hungry and thirsty enough, he'd pull loose. By then Slocum would be back—or he wouldn't be coming back.

He went forward on foot, creeping cautiously through the dark, alert to any sounds ahead. A chill wind whipped across the prairie, rustling the grass and making Slocum's work a little easier. Finally he heard them: the guttural sounds of male voices. He smelled smoke. They'd made campfires, tiny ones of buffalo dung, and they'd hidden them in the creek bed, so that close as he was, Slocum saw only the faintest sign of light.

The lords of the plains had come to roost for the night.

Slocum decided he was already too close. At least he had them located. As carefully as he'd come, he crept back to where he'd left his horse and then walked him a mile before he mounted.

He rode back down his own trail. Presently he saw a light, long before he heard voices. Someone didn't care if he was seen.

"Ho," he called. "Cavanaugh?"

The voice nearby startled him. He'd not seen or heard the night guard. "Slocum?" it called.

"Right."

"Go on in."

Slocum rode past the invisible guard. There were seven men camped in a fold of the rolling prairie. As Slocum came in, Cavanaugh stood. "Got too dark to follow your signs," he said. "Slocum, this is Billy Dixon. He's the leader of this hunting party."

Cavanaugh indicated a man in his early twenties. He wore a straggly mustache, and his clothes, like those of all the buffalo hunters, were made entirely of leather. Dixon examined Slocum for a moment, then nodded. "Get down," he said. "Have some hot coffee. You find them Comanche?"

"Yeah." Slocum swung down and went to the campfire. "Yeah, they're camped about four, five miles west of here. Didn't get a close look, but it's got to be the same party."

"You didn't see the girl, then?" Dixon asked.

"Didn't get that close. You know her?"

"Some," Dixon said. "Cracker MacFarlane and his partners have been out here awhile. Hauled hides for us, some. Then all of a sudden they were headed west. Wouldn't say why. Going to California in one all-fired hurry. Looked safe enough. Haven't seen a Comanche in a month. Figured they were all down toward *la jornada del muerto* to trade. It's the right season." Dixon took the bandanna from his neck and used it to snag the coffee pot from the fire. He took a tin cup from the ground, poured in some coffee to swill around and wash the cup, threw that away, and poured the cup full. "Reckon you could use some of this," he said.

"Sure can. Thanks." Slocum sipped at the hot liquid.

The others sat impassively around the fire, not speaking until Dixon was through. Slocum looked them over and had an impulse to laugh. The representatives of civilization. They all wore leather clothing, mostly stained with dried blood from skinning buffalo. They smelled to high heaven, even through a dung fire. Not one of them had shaved in a month.

But by God they were here because they were needed, and Slocum was damned glad to see them.

"This here's my crew," Dixon said. "My partner, Bill Masterson. Some call him Bat." He indicated a man even younger than himself, younger than twenty. Masterson waved. "And Dirty-face Ike, Three Fingers, Ben Dobbs, Prairie Dog Jack. Dutch Henry you met. He's out on guard."

Slocum nodded to each. The men were all ages. Prairie Dog Jack looked to be sixty, maybe older. They were all sizes, and all were worn hard from life on the plains. A tough breed. "Glad to see you all," Slocum said.

" 'You all.' A gray-pants," Three Fingers muttered. "You ride out this way in the war?"

Slocum shook his head. "Army of Virginia, mostly. You?"

"Quantrill," Three Fingers said. "Rest of 'em here was blue-britches, 'cept for couple too young to be in the war."

"Wish I had been," Slocum said.

"Me too. You got any thoughts on this situation?" Three Fingers asked.

"Hell," Dixon said. "There's what, a dozen of the bastards? Nine of us. Not bad odds. Maybe we should just ride in there."

"Not good," Slocum said. "They'd kill the girl for sure."

"Likely," Dixon agreed. "Maybe she'd rather it be that way." He fished into his pocket and came out with a hard ball of what looked like wax, about the size of a walnut. "My bite. Cyanide. We all got one. Doc back at Fort Dodge says one bite on that wax bullet and you're a goner. I keep it just in case them Kiowa or Comanche are likely to get me. Rather go that way than how they'd send me."

Slocum, remembering the man lashed to the wagon wheel, and MacFarlane, blinded and crippled, could only agree and wish he had one of the wax bullets. Just in case.

"If that's how she wants it," Slocum said, "you can give her that. But maybe we ought to ask her first, instead of making sure they put a knife in her ribs. Hell, maybe they didn't hurt her at all. Sometimes they sell kids to the Comanchero. When I rode with the Fourth Cav, we bought back half a dozen kids from the Comancheros."

"Yeah." Dixon spat into the fire. "You know, them's the bastards I hate. Comancheros. Hell, the Comanche, they belong out here; they can't help how they live. But them greaser Comancheros—sell guns to the savages, sell ammunition, sell kids, help kill white people just for money—them's the ones I'd like to blow all to hell. Every one of them." Dixon spat again.

"We must do something," Cavanaugh said. "We have to get her out of there."

"You know her?" Dixon asked.

"No. But she's a white girl."

"True," Bat Masterson said. He spoke low and easy, a young man with a lot of confidence in himself. "We have to get her out of there. But that's not going to be easy. Cracker MacFarlane's bunch were mucho-tough hombres. Any bunch that could kill old Cracker is not going to be easy."

"He must have got careless," Dixon said. "He sure was in one all-fired hurry to get west all of a sudden."

"How old is the girl?" Slocum asked.

"About nineteen," Masterson said. "Pretty girl. Old Cracker wasn't really her father."

"If the girl is that old, it's likely they've all taken turns with her," Slocum said. He drank the last of his coffee and spat into the fire.

"Damn it, don't talk like that," Prairie Dog Jack said. He squirmed uncomfortably. "Damn."

"Maybe one took a fancy to her and kept her for himself," Dixon said.

"Yeah. Girl always was a little crazy," Masterson said. "Wonder what it does to a girl's mind, having a bunch take turns like that."

"Hey, hold on," Three Fingers protested. "She's a nice kid."

"Sure," Masterson said. "I know that. But you heard her. Always dreaming. Talking about how she's going to be rich someday." Masterson laughed. "Rich, hell. Cracker MacFarlane never did have a hundred dollars to his name. But Laura kept talking about how someday her daddy would send for her; she'd leave Cracker and go west—"

Three Fingers shrugged. "Don't much blame her for that. Old Cracker wanted that girl so bad you could see it a mile away. Hadn't been for Miz Mary—" He grinned in the firelight. " 'Course, Mary couldn't have been watchin' *all* the time."

"Cracker never got Laura," Masterson said. "Sure, he had an ache, but he treated her better'n he would if she'd been his real daughter."

"Suit yourself," Three Fingers said. "With Cracker you never could be sure. Hell, he'd have fucked a sidewinder if somebody'd hold its head."

"Not Laura," Masterson said. "There wasn't a one of us wouldn't have liked to take her into his blanket roll, but nobody ever did. That Miz Mary was the meanest woman I ever saw. Wonder what the Comanches saw in her."

"Talkin' ill of the dead never did any good," Billy Dixon said. The others nodded agreement.

"Yeah," Masterson said. "Besides, Laura was different. Like a real lady. Never let on to knowin' what you were talkin' about. Seems she grew up that way, not to know about men and women."

"Reckon she knows now." Ben Dobbs was older, closer to Slocum's age than to Dixon and Masterson's. "What are we sittin' here for? We got to do something."

"What?" Three Fingers asked.

"Sure are a lot of Comanche," Masterson said. "I count fifteen from the sign. Slocum?"

"About that," Slocum agreed.

"Too damn many," Masterson said. "Ever try sneakin' into a Comanche camp at night, Ben?" he asked Dobbs.

"I've done it," Ben Dobbs said.

"Then you're the only man who ever did."

"You callin' me a liar?" Dobbs demanded.

Masterson shook his head, but his eyes narrowed, and his hand hovered near his hip. "Nope. I just never heard of anybody doin' that."

"Keep it peaceful," Dixon said. "Bat, he's got the coup stick to prove it. Took it right out of a Comanche raiding camp on a bet."

Masterson shrugged and relaxed. "Well, Dobbs maybe can do that, but I sure as hell can't. Anybody else think they can?"

Nobody spoke for a moment. "What matter does it make?" Slocum asked. "Even if we could get in there, we wouldn't be able to find the girl before one of 'em puts a knife in her ribs."

"I hate to think what they're doin' to her. Right now." Ben Dobbs licked his thin lips. "Right now."

"What do we fight with once we get close?" Dixon demanded. He patted his long buffalo gun. "Anniemarie here can knock down a bull buff'ler at half a mile, but she sure don't load too fast." Lovingly he stroked the thick octagon barrel.

All the hunters carried them, big Sharps single-shot rifles that threw a slug half an inch around. Most of the weapons were fitted with small brass telescopes for sights, and each had a folding iron rod attached to the barrel, a rest to swing down to steady the piece. They weren't handy weapons for close-up fighting.

"Sure like to kill 'em at night," Ben Dobbs said. "Like to think of 'em wanderin' forever, never findin' their huntin' ground. God damn if I don't like killin' 'em at night better'n skinnin' the bastards alive."

Slocum poured more coffee and blew on it for it to cool. He'd been thinking along those lines himself, but there was no getting around it: the hunters weren't armed for a close-up fight, and sneaking into a Comanche trail camp wasn't anything you wanted to do. Slocum thought he had a good chance of getting up close, but it was a risk, and he wasn't willing to try without a damned good reason. The lords of the plains kept good watch, and they might not like to fight at night, but they sure as hell could do it.

And the first thing they'd do would be to put a knife in the girl.

"I like killin' 'em at night, too," Slocum said. "But maybe there's a better way. I thought up a plan."

IV

The half moon was gibbous and yellow. Thin clouds scudded across its face. Slocum crawled through the buffalo grass, feeling every inch of the way before he moved, slithering on his belly and making only a few yards each hour. Somewhere off to his left Ben Dobbs was doing the same thing.

The Comanche camp was still, the only sound the movement of the ponies picketed about fifty yards from their campsite. The Comanches were sure to have their horses guarded. Horse-stealing was their favorite occupation, and any other band of Indians out on the trail might try to run off with the ponies. Slocum was crawling in from the other side, moving slowly and carefully, avoiding the dry patches that might rustle and give him away. Every few yards he lay perfectly still to listen.

Eventually he heard another sound—soft movement off to his left and ahead. Slocum parted the grass carefully to look through in the moonlight. Forty yards away a Comanche sat, motionless as a statue.

That would be the camp guard. There wasn't a chance in hell of slipping up on him. Slocum didn't think there was a man alive who could do that. He was sure that man wasn't him. He wasn't trying it. Too big a chance to take. What Slocum had to do was get in position for the morning.

He moved carefully to his right, circling away from the seated watchman. He hoped Ben Dobbs was as good as he claimed to be and that he'd spotted the watching Indian.

There was another sound—louder this time, and not far ahead. Slocum decided he'd gone far enough. It wouldn't do to get right in with the Comanche. He lay down to wait for dawn.

Out behind him the other hunters, and Cavanaugh, would be circling the camp to get west of it. They wouldn't come closer than half a mile.

The sounds ahead were louder, and mingled with another: a man's grunts, and another voice, high-pitched and breathless. "Oh. Oh. Oh."

A woman being loved. Her moans were a mixture of terror and pain and something else as her body responded to the repeated thrusts of the Comanche brave.

God damn, Slocum thought.

The Indian grunted harder, faster. Slocum drew his Bowie knife and crawled forward. That was one Comanche who wasn't listening. The noise would cover Slocum's movements, and he could go faster. He slithered forward until he could see.

The Comanches had made a trail camp, no tepees or shelter, only buffalo hides spread on the ground with buffalo robes laid on the hides. Just ahead was one of the beds, and the robe was humping up and down, fast.

Enjoy yourself, you son of a bitch, Slocum thought. It's the last fuck you'll ever have.

He moved forward until he was next to the robe. The brave was grunting, and the girl's cries came faster. Slocum looked around. He couldn't see any others nearby. This must be a brave who'd bought, or won, the girl, and he'd camped off to the side away from the others so he could enjoy his prize in privacy.

Slocum took the edge of the robe in his left hand and raised the Bowie knife. He pulled back the robe.

The Indian's head was just where Slocum thought it would be. The buck turned toward him, still not understanding, his eyes filled with rage. He just had time to see that it wasn't one of his companions who'd raised his blanket before Slocum drove the point of the Bowie into the back of his neck.

The buck screamed, but it sounded like lust. There were sniggers from the other side of the camp.

As the Indian died, Slocum clapped his hand over the girl's mouth. Her eyes were wide with terror.

"It's all right," Slocum whispered. He put his mouth

to her ear. "We came to get you out of here. It's all right."

The girl struggled for a moment, still not comprehending; then she went limp. Slocum released her mouth. She lay panting, but she didn't say anything. Slocum pushed the dead Comanche off her and crawled in next to her under the robe. Then he pulled the buffalo robe up over his head.

He put his mouth next to her ear again. "Ma'am, I hate to talk about it, but I have to know. Do they take turns with you, or was this one the only one likely to use this bed tonight?"

She drew in a breath, and Slocum clapped his hand over her mouth again. "Soft," he warned. "They find me here, we're both finished."

She nodded, and he released her. "He's the only one," the girl said. "He was the leader." Her voice dissolved into sobs. She began to cry hopelessly.

Slocum put his arms around her. She was a tiny girl, not more than five feet tall, and very slenderly built. He could feel her naked flesh against him, and her breasts against his chest felt full and hard—a woman's breasts, not those of a little girl. A woman, naked, and he was in bed with her. He felt his manhood grow hard, and was ashamed of himself.

The girl held him, her head against his shoulder, and cried. He lay that way, huddled against the crying naked girl and the stiffening dead Indian, until dawn.

Slocum used his knife to open a peephole in the robe. He lay still, the dead Comanche pulled close to them, hoping none of the other braves would look too close. Outside there was faint light, not really enough to see far. This would be the tricky part.

The girl lay against him, too exhausted to cry anymore. She wasn't quite asleep, but she lay like the dead. Poor kid, Slocum thought. What the hell happens to her now? There wasn't a chance in the world that one of the others wouldn't tell this story, and she'd be marked for life. Girl raped by the Indians. Some would think she ought to kill herself. If she doesn't, Slocum thought, there'll be plenty who'll figure she's fair game.

It wasn't an attitude that made any sense, but it was widespread. Women were either ladies or whores out here, and Laura MacFarlane sure as hell wasn't going to be thought of as a lady, not after this.

Outside there was more light. The others were stirring. Slocum clutched his rifle. When the sun was a little stronger, when the camp would be framed against the light while the men to the west were still in darkness—

There was the heavy, booming crash of a Sharps rifle, then another, then several together as the hunters fired off a ragged volley. Horses screamed in pain and terror. There were shouts of rage and hatred from the Indian camp.

The girl jerked and screamed. Slocum grabbed her and forced her to lie still. He kept the covers over his head and peeked out through the hole he'd made. The camp was a boil of activity. Slocum brought up his Colt pistol and aimed at the closest Comanche through the slit in the robe. He fired, and the brave spun and fell with a bewildered look.

The Comanche weren't looking toward Slocum. They were all running toward their horses.

Six of the ponies were down. There was another crash as the hunters fired a second volley of half-inch balls. Pushed by one hundred ten grains of powder, the Sharps rifles could knock down a buffalo at eight hundred yards.

Buffalo weren't the target this morning. Today the hunters were shooting down Indian ponies. They hadn't dared try to shoot the sleeping Indians. The Comanche didn't camp in plain view, and even if they could see them, there'd have been no way to know where the girl was; but the horses were visible in the morning light and made a good target.

Slocum threw back the buffalo robe and stood with his rifle ready. The Indians were still running to save their ponies. Even as they ran, two more horses reared in pain, rising and prancing their death agony, both hit by a single ball that passed through one and embedded itself in the next one's ribs. The Sharps rifles crashed again and again, and the last of the ponies reared and fell.

Every horse was down. The lords of the plains were on foot.

They hadn't expected that. Horse-stealing was an honorable profession among all plains Indians, but senseless slaughter of good horses was beyond their comprehension. They had guarded their mounts against theft, but nothing could guard them from a Sharps at eight hundred yards.

Slocum rushed forward. He could see Ben Dobbs now, about forty yards to his left, and behind him, maybe fifty yards from the camp, Jim Cavanaugh was rushing up. Slocum couldn't see any other white men. The buffalo hunters would be out there somewhere, kneeling in the grass to the west, with the Indians backlighted against the rising sun. Once again the deadly Sharps rifles crashed, and two Indians fell.

The Comanche saw Slocum, and half a dozen warriors ran toward him. As Slocum had guessed, these were all young braves, none older than twenty. The man he'd killed under the blanket was no older, and he'd been the leader. This was probably their first pony-stealing raid, a raid to prove their manhood and skills.

The fastest of them rushed at him, and Slocum brought up the Winchester and fired into the running warrior's chest. The Comanche went down with a shout of rage and defiance. Slocum worked the lever and fired rapidly as the others closed. He heard the girl scream behind him and turned to see a Comanche moving close with a rifle. Slocum fired, missed in his haste, and fired again. The Indian staggered.

Cavanaugh had run into the camp. He worked the lever of his Henry rifle like a madman, firing rapidly at the Indians but not making many hits. A brave charged the drummer with an ax, and Slocum shot him down just before he reached Cavanaugh. Cavanaugh waved his rifle in acknowledgment.

The camp was boiling with Indians, and there were only the three of them—Slocum, Cavanaugh, and Dobbs—to face them. At half a mile's range, a man could run ten yards in the time it took a slug to travel to him, and these Indians were all running. The long-range riflemen wouldn't be much more help.

Slocum was surrounded. He felt a lance strike at him, felt the steel tip grate along his ribs, felt the quick, searing pain. He glanced down and saw the bright-red blood seeping from his side, but he had no time to see how badly he was hurt.

The lance struck at him again and Slocum parried with the rifle. He tried to work the lever and still avoid the sharp, iron-tipped lance. The lancer moved back a step, skillfully changing the angle of his thrust, and charged as Slocum tried to lever a shell.

Slocum felt the cartridge tear and knew the extractor had ripped it apart. The rifle was hopelessly jammed. It would take five minutes to get the spent shell out of the chamber, and Slocum didn't have five seconds. It was common enough. Many a trooper had died because of poor ammunition and a jammed weapon.

Slocum swung the rifle desperately and batted the thrusting lance aside. The lancer grinned. He knew.

The lance moved forward once more, and the lancer's face dissolved in red. Slocum looked over to see Cavanaugh levering another shell into his weapon. They grinned at each other. "Score's even," Slocum called. He swung the stock of his useless rifle at another charging Comanche, then dropped the rifle and drew his Navy .36, thumbing back the hammer with a smooth motion, as he'd been teaching himself. An Indian was almost upon him with a knife, and Slocum thrust the pistol forward and fired with the muzzle almost touching his enemy. The ball went through the Comanche warrior's lungs. The Indian coughed blood and staggered back a step, but he didn't go down. He drew a club from his belt and swung the stone head at Slocum.

John dodged, dropped to one knee to get under the swing, and fired again. This time the Indian fell, but there was another to take his place, and another coming up from behind. Slocum fired once more, then leaped to his feet and sprinted back to the bedding where the girl lay. A brave stood over the buffalo robe with a trade tomahawk, a steel combat ax made in the east for sale to the Indians.

Slocum pulled the trigger and heard the hammer fall on a bad cap. He thumbed the weapon and fired again. This time it went off, and the Comanche's head blew apart like a ripe watermelon. His brains sprayed across the camp, and he fell, still holding his ax.

There were five more braves in the campsite that Slocum could see. One was standing over Ben Dobbs. Slocum hadn't seen the hunter go down, but now he lay still on the ground. Cavanaugh fired twice, and the man who'd killed Dobbs fell across the hunter's body.

Two others closed on Slocum. The nearest one spurted blood from a ruined left shoulder. The wound was large enough to put two fingers in, a terrible wound torn by a Sharps .50, but still the brave ran toward Slocum. He held a pistol in his right hand, and he fired recklessly until Slocum shot him down. The brave fell into the ashes of the campfire and lay writhing, still trying to aim his pistol at Slocum.

John's pistol was empty. He holstered the weapon and drew his Bowie knife as another brave leaped toward him with a knife. Slocum wished for a cavalry saber. The things were noisy and generally useless, but for close fighting when the ammunition was gone there was no better weapon.

He parried the brave's first thrust with the Bowie, hanging the Indian's blade against the brass backing until he could shift his weight to get back on balance. The warrior jumped back, then made another rush, feinting with the blade before trying a kick. Slocum dodged and kicked toward the Indian's balls. The brave turned to catch the blow on his leg and came forward again, his blade moving in intricate, tricky passes, knife hand held low.

They train at this all their lives, Slocum thought. No matter how good you think you are, they practice this more than you ever will.

Slocum swayed backward in a classic saber retreat, then lunged with the point aimed at the other's face. When the Comanche reacted, Slocum brought the Bowie around in a saberman's *moulinet* and thrust toward the brave's outstretched arm. He felt the sharp steel connect and saw blood spurt, but the Indian didn't drop his knife.

Not good enough. Slocum had hit the bone, but the brave gritted his teeth and ignored it. They circled warily now. Slocum saw respect in his enemy's eyes. Respect, but no fear. The Comanche lunged again. Slocum stepped into the attack to bat the approaching knife aside, continued with a classic *riposte*. His left hand grasped frantically for the Indian's blade wrist.

Slocum's fingers touched, grasped, clamped on the Indian's wrist. The arm was slippery with blood, and it was hard to get a grip. He felt strong fingers at his own right hand, and they stood straining at each other, each holding the other's blade hand. It had become a contest of pure animal strength, and Slocum felt the other's power.

The Comanche swept a kick toward Slocum's knee. John twisted, catching the moccasin on the side of his leg. It hurt like hell, and Slocum braced to keep from falling. Slowly he felt his left hand being forced inward, as the Comanche's blade came closer, its point touching Slocum's ribs, while John's own blade seemed embedded in an anvil, so strong was the brave's grip.

He saw movement from the corner of his eye. Someone was moving toward them. Slocum had no attention to spare. If that was another Indian coming, Slocum was finished, no question about it; but there wasn't a damn thing he could do except hang on, push with his right and strain against the Indian's thrusts with his left, hold the deadly point away from his ribs and hope he'd last longer than the warrior he faced. He wasn't sure he could do it.

Suddenly the steel grip on Slocum's right hand was gone. His Bowie snapped in and the point buried itself in the Comanche's back, tearing upward into the kidneys. The brave's knees buckled and his eyes went dim. He slumped to the ground.

The girl stood beside the warrior. She was still stark naked. She held a Comanche war club in both hands, and she'd used it to crack the brave's skull. Now, as he fell, she struck at him again and again, flailing at him until the brave was stretched out on the ground, and still she struck, at his head, at his body, his face, his testicles, smashing repeatedly at the bloody hulk there on the ground. She screamed continually, a wordless keening of rage and pain and hate.

Slocum turned. There was one more Comanche nearby. His chest was bloody and he lay on the ground, but he had a pistol, and its muzzle was swinging toward John Slocum. Slocum flipped his Bowie knife upward and threw it at the brave. The knife flew straight and true toward the fallen Indian, but it was going to be too late. The pistol was pointing at Slocum, the muzzle as wide as death. Slocum heard a shot.

It took him a moment to realize that he hadn't been hit. The Comanche warrior lay still, Slocum's knife in his chest. He had never fired his weapon. Jim Cavanaugh stood nearby with his rifle, and the Indian had a new mouth, a gaping hole in his throat were Cavanaugh had shot him.

"Reckon that's the last of them," Cavanaugh shouted. "We've given those bastards the bill."

The naked girl continued to scream in rage. She ran from one body to the next and pounded each with her war club, smashing their heads and bodies and testicles into sticky red jelly.

V

"Laura!" Slocum shouted. "Laura MacFarlane!"

She smashed at another body, then hesitated at the sound. She turned toward Slocum and Cavanaugh. Her eyes blazed. She moved toward them like a sleepwalker, and she carried the war club upraised. It was made of two feet of oak sapling, decorated with leather thongs, and was topped by a buckskin-wrapped, smooth, round river rock that weighed more than a pound. It could crack skulls like walnuts. She moved closer to Slocum, still swinging the club.

John dodged. "Hey!" he shouted. "We're friends. It's over!"

The mad light slowly died from her eyes. She looked puzzled for a moment. "My name is not MacFarlane!" she screamed. "Not MacFarlane!" Then she realized where she was, standing stark mother naked with a bloody club in her hand, her legs spattered with blood. She stared at the club and at the battered bodies of the Comanches, then at Slocum and Cavanaugh and the buffalo hunters running into the camp. The club swayed and fell to the ground. Her knees gave.

Slocum caught her as she fell. She clung to him, recognizing him as the man who'd stayed with her all night. She held him tightly and sobbed uncontrollably.

Jim Cavanaugh took off his coat and put it around her. After a moment she huddled into it. The racking sobs died away. "Thank you," she said. "Thank you for coming for me."

The hunters came in yelling in triumph. "Whoo-ee!" Billy Dixon yelled. "What a hell of a fight! Fourteen dead Comanche!" There were shots from over near the picket lines where the horses lay. "Well, soon to be dead, anyway." Dixon stopped at Ben Dobbs's body. He bent over, straightened, his grin fading but not gone. "Too bad about Ben."

Cavanaugh searched around the buffalo robes until he found Laura's skirt and blouse. He brought them over. "Here, ma'am. I reckon you ought to put these on."

She nodded and began dressing. The men looked away, but their looks were puzzled. They'd known her as a girl, old enough to be a woman but not really grown up. They didn't really recognize her now, this fully formed woman naked in the camp. They couldn't forget what had happened to her, and their eyes showed it.

She saw their looks and huddled near Slocum again. There was blood on her hand after she touched him, and she stared at it. "You're hurt," she said.

The lance wound on his left side was hurting him. So was his bruised leg, but that would take care of itself. Something had to be done about the gouge along his ribs.

Dutch Henry came in leading the horses. Slocum limped over to Dorkus.

"I'll fix that," Laura said. She ran to the horses. "Do any of you have soap?" she asked.

Slocum looked at Bat Masterson. The young hunter was grinning in triumph. "Does she always talk that way?" Slocum asked.

"How?"

"Stiff. Educated."

"Yeah. She didn't grow up out here, that's for sure. She tried to tell me once, few years ago, about how she'd grown up in Richmond, but Miz Mary didn't like her talking to men."

Dutch Henry fished into his saddle bags and came up with a thick bar of yellow laundry soap. Laura took it and a canteen and went back to Slocum. "Take off your shirt," she said. Her voice seemed very calm now, not the frightened sobs they'd heard before.

She made a lather with the soap and washed off Slocum's side while John stood stiffly and hissed to keep from yelling. It hurt like hell. When she had it cleaned, he looked at the wound. The lance had scraped along his ribs and gouged out a chunk of meat half an inch wide and at least as deep. It ran all across his left side at the rib line. A flap of loose skin hung from it.

She took his Bowie knife from the sheath, tested the edged, and washed it off. Then she carved away the loose patch of skin and made a thicker lather from the soap, peeled off part of the bar, and packed soap in to fill the gap where the meat had come out. Slocum gritted his teeth and let her work.

He approved of the treatment. Some of his troopers, in both the Confederate and Yankee armies, had sworn by laundry soap. Surgeons didn't know what made a wound fester, but sometimes even a small one, a scratch—nothing bad at all—would turn green and get full of pus and start to stink, and then the red streaks would move toward the heart. Blood poisoning. Or the wound would become gangrenous and the man would rot to death. Nobody knew what caused it, but Slocum had noticed that troopers who used laundry soap usually recovered and that a lot of them who went to field hospitals didn't.

Billy Dixon went out to count bodies. He came back nodding with satisfaction. "Got them all," he said. "Fourteen horses, fourteen bodies." They were all grinning in triumph, a little foolishly. "That was one sweet fight," Dixon said. "Slocum, you'll do. Yes, sir, you'll plain do."

The hunters went around the campsite collecting trophies: coup sticks, axes, knives, the worn guns, but also the little medicine bags the Indians had worn. Trophies, Slocum thought. The Indians take scalps; we take trophies. He'd known white men who took scalps.

He didn't say anything. One of the hunters might lift scalps if anybody talked about it, and that didn't seem like the right thing to do. Slocum didn't want to try explaining the difference between people and savages, not to these plains warriors. Maybe there wasn't much difference to begin with. No Indian had ever taken scalps until an English officer chanced on this handy device for tallying the kills during one of the endless French-English struggles that always spilled over into a Canadian-American conflict. Damn Europe and its wars! Didn't this continent have violence enough of its own? He laughed bitterly. He'd been part of yet another European venture, Maximilian's abortive Empire of Mexico.

Suddenly the whole scene made him ill, and he wanted to get away. Laura had borrowed a needle and thread from Cavanaugh and was patching up Slocum's shirt. She had it almost done. Slocum found his rifle and worked at it until he had the torn cartridge out of the chamber. He loaded it and tested the action and feed to be sure it was working again. Then he took out powder and balls and caps and reloaded the Navy .36, smearing buffalo fat on top of the balls to make sure dust and water couldn't get in there.

Cavanaugh was doing the same thing. "They tell me Colonel Colt is making a cartridge pistol," the drummer said. "Shoots regular cartridges like a repeating rifle."

"I've heard of it," Slocum said. He went over to retrieve his shirt. His body was covered with scars from the war. Now he'd have another one. "Thanks, Miss Laura," he said when he got his shirt.

She tried to smile, but her face showed misery and fear when she turned to him. "I don't know how to thank you—"

"It's all right. You're not hurt?"

"Not wounded," she said.

There wasn't much Slocum could say to that. He buttoned up the shirt and whistled up Dorkus. He stood ready to mount. "Reckon I'll get on down the way," he said.

"You'd be welcome to come back to camp with us," Billy Dixon said. "Join up with us on shares. Ever skin buffalo? We could use another partner, now that Ben Dobbs is dead."

"I've shot buffalo," Slocum said. He considered the proposition, then shook his head. He had no place to go, but buffalo hunting was a sad business. "Reckon I'll head on to Santa Fe."

Laura ran to him in sudden decision. "Take me with you!" she said.

"Now, Miss Laura," Billy Dixon protested. "You should stay with us—"

"I do not belong here," she said. "I never have. I stayed with Sergeant MacFarlane because—because I had to. But now I must go to California. Please, Mr. Slocum, let me come with you as far as Santa Fe."

Jim Cavanaugh was saddling up. He turned toward them. "I'll be heading west after I make my rounds in Santa Fe," he said. "You could come with me."

"I want to stay with Slocum," she said.

Cavanaugh shrugged. "We can all go together. Far as Santa Fe, anyway."

Bat Masterson came over to Slocum. He spoke quietly, his voice not carrying far enough for anyone else to hear. He looked and sounded a lot older than his nineteen years. "Slocum, it'd be best if you did take her with you. There'd be no other women in camp, and we won't be going back to Dodge for a while. I don't rightly know what'd happen, one girl in a camp full of men out on the plains. We all know what happened to her. We all know, and we'd get to thinking about it, and hell, I'm not even sure I trust myself. It'd be best if she went with you. She can take Ben's mule and gear. Ben for sure won't be needin' them."

"Please," Laura said again. She looked small and helpless, but Slocum couldn't help remembering the grown woman's breasts under the calico blouse and the blond triangle between her legs.

"I'm not so sure you can trust me," Slocum said.

"I don't care."

"Why with me?"

"Because . . . because I felt safe after I . . . after we met," she said. "Because you didn't hurt me."

"But hell—"

"I have to find my relatives," she said. "If I have to, I'll go to Santa Fe alone."

"Oh, hell, come on with me," Slocum said.

"Thank you."

"She's got some money coming," Billy Dixon said.

"We found what they took off Cracker. Couple of hundred dollars." He held out a small leather pouch. It clinked. "Least it was on a dead Comanche, and that's Cracker's poke, so I can't think who's got a better title. That'll be more'n enough to buy her a stage ticket."

"I'll get Ben's mule," Masterson said. He sounded relieved and disappointed at the same time. Slocum knew how they felt. Decency caused them to send her away, but they were already regretting it.

Jim Cavanaugh came over. "Be best if we all three ride to Santa Fe," he said. "Maybe more Comanche out there."

"All right," Slocum said. By nature a loner, he didn't care for all this company, but it made sense. "Let's get moving. I want to make some miles." He touched his left side. It was sure as hell going to hurt tomorrow. Come to that, it didn't feel so good today. He turned to Laura. "We'll be moving pretty fast. Can you keep up?"

This time her laugh was almost genuine. "Mr. Slocum, I grew up with horses. Of course I can ride. Even on a mule."

Slocum considered how torn and bleeding she must be, but there was no way to talk about that.

"She can ride with the best of them," Billy Dixon agreed. "Good to have met you, Slocum."

"You, too." Slocum waved to the buffalo hunters. He swung into the saddle, wincing at the pain in his side, and turned to Laura and Cavanaugh. "Let's make some miles."

VI

They rode hard. Slocum soon found that Laura hadn't been wrong. She rode with shortened stirrups, practically standing in the saddle to relieve the pain she had to be feeling, but she didn't complain. She could ride. Ben Dobbs's long-legged mule, steadier than most horses, trotted alongside Dorkus with no trouble at all, easily keeping up, while Cavanaugh tended to fall behind.

The plains stretched endlessly before them. The hills ahead seemed to come no closer. At dusk, with the sun setting behind the mountains, it looked as if you could reach out and touch those hills, but in the morning the mountains had crawled away again.

When they made camp the first night, Laura slept near Slocum. He could feel her presence, and wondered what he might do if Cavanaugh had not been there. The memory of her naked under the buffalo robe haunted him until he slept; with the memory came shame. She was only a young woman raped by the Comanche, and he had no call to think of her any other way.

But he did.

When they rode out the second day, his ribs ached badly, and they were nearly as bad on the third. The pain alone would have been enough to keep him from talking much, and they rode hard enough that when they made cold camp at night, they fell into bed without much conversation. Slocum wasn't happy letting Cavanaugh sit guard, although the man seemed competent enough, and John dozed fitfully until it was his turn. Then he wouldn't call Cavanaugh but would sit all night, so that by the time they reached the foothills of the Rockies, Slocum was nearly asleep in the saddle.

He woke stiff and plain tuckered out. Cavanaugh broke camp, and Slocum waited until the other two were saddled up. "You got your machinery to sell," Slocum said. "You two go on. I think I'll give Dorkus a rest, take it easy. I'm in no hurry."

Cavanaugh shrugged. "Okay by me. I expect it's safe enough along the road from here."

"I'll stay with you," Laura said. "If you don't mind."

Slocum didn't care much for company, but the girl had already dismounted and was loosening the cinch on the mule. "I thought you were in a hurry."

Cavanaugh suddenly looked like a man who'd opened a three-minute egg and found a three-minute embryo. "I thought you were riding on to Santa Fe," he said. His voice was an accusation.

"I'll be all right." There was finality in Laura's tone.

Cavanaugh gave Slocum a goatish wink. "Too bad I can't stay with you," he said. Then he shrugged. "See you around."

"Sure. Had us some good shooting back in that Comanche camp. My thanks to you," Slocum said. And just why was Cavanaugh acting like this? Sweet on the girl? That didn't make a lot of sense. There'd be plenty of women in Santa Fe.

"Sure." Cavanaugh looked wistfully at Laura again. Then he clucked his horse forward and turned down the road for Santa Fe.

They watched the drummer ride away. Slocum used the morning to clean his weapons, mend saddle gear, and just take it easy while Dorkus grazed on the greener grass at the edge of the prairie. Laura sat quietly, not in the way, not trying to talk. She wasn't hard to have around.

Maybe she wants something else, Slocum thought. He pushed that thought away.

It was midafternoon when they moved on. The stage road wound along the base of the foothills and high peaks. It was as if a line had been drawn across the land, hills on one side, plains on the other. Instead of dying grass and dust there were wildflowers and greenery to ride through, and not far above were stands of pine. A stream ran down from the mountains above.

They made camp early and plunged into the stream, clothes and all, to wash off the trail dust. Slocum stayed downstream to give Laura privacy. He washed thoroughly and hung out his clothes, putting on his spare trousers. He had no spare shirt. He got out a blanket and spread it near a large boulder and lay down to relax in the warmth of the sun.

After a while she came out to join him. Her wet dress clung to her body, showing every detail of her small but perfectly formed breasts, the gentle curve of her hips. A woman's body, Slocum thought, not for the first time. Tiny, but a full-grown woman. He turned away before he thought about that any longer. Unwanted memories came to him again.

She sat, silently chewing the end of a rye stalk. There were peaceful sounds from the stream and the song of a lark nearby. The late-afternoon sun warmed them, and so did the heat from the boulder.

"I wish we could stay here forever," she said.

"It's peaceful. We'll stay the night, anyway."

She was silent for a long moment. "John?"

"Yes?"

"Where will you go now?"

He shrugged. "Beats me."

"Might you go to California?"

"Hadn't thought to. Haven't thought much beyond Santa Fe."

"But where are you going?"

"Drifting. Looking for something. Not sure what."

"You have no home either," she said.

"Had a place once. Gone now."

She nodded. "The war. Our home was burned. John, come with me to California."

"What's there?"

"They say things are better out there. That you can forget the war and start over."

"They do say that. You've got kinfolk there?"

"I think so." Her voice was small and full of doubts. "It's hard to remember. I was only twelve when the war ended. My father sent me off with Sergeant Mac-

Farlane, just before Richmond fell. We were going to go to California then, but we didn't."

"You heard from your daddy since?"

"Not often. Some."

"Doesn't seem he was too interested," Slocum said.

"That's not fair. There were reasons," Laura said. "He couldn't write to me before. And now I have to find him."

"Reasons," Slocum said.

"It's not my story to tell," Laura said. "At first we were hiding from the Pinkertons. Cracker kept us moving all the time, always going west."

"Pinks must have wanted you pretty bad," Slocum said.

"They did. And then—then there wasn't any reason for them to follow us, but we didn't hear, and then we got the letter telling where to meet him and we started west, and—" She shuddered at the memory. Her voice fell to a whisper. "The story will get around, won't it? And everyone will look at me the way—the way Billy Dixon and Bat Masterson and the others looked at me. The way they look at dance-hall women."

"Maybe not," Slocum said. "No reason why the story needs to get further west. Nobody out this way knows but Cavanaugh and me, and no reason for either one of us to talk about it."

"I hope you're right." She sighed. "It's a long way to California. I know what I'm looking for is gone, with Virginia and the South. It's all gone now, but there must be something else. There must be something. Maybe I'll find it in California."

"Sure." Slocum rolled over onto his back and looked up at fleecy clouds racing high in the sky above. Down at ground level there was no wind at all. The sun was warm and lazy. Sure, he thought. Sure, there has to be something, but there won't be. It's all gone, along with home. All gone.

"Was your house burned?" Laura asked.

"No. Carpetbaggers took it."

"And you couldn't get it back?"

Slocum shrugged. "Tried. Ended in a gunfight. I killed two men, father and son. There are three brothers left. They set the law on me, and looked for me a long time. Guess they'll still be looking."

"Can't you go back?"

"Maybe. Southern jury won't look too hard at dead carpetbaggers, now that there are state courts again. But there's nothing to go back to. Place has been sold a couple of times. Sisters are married, folks are dead, and what would I do? No, can't go back." He stared at the clouds again. "Maybe you're right. Maybe there's something in California." And you have to believe in it, he thought.

She was silent again. He saw her shudder and didn't say anything.

"Please don't look at me," she said. "Just let me talk." She sat staring at her feet, not looking at Slocum. "I remember when my sister was married. I was about ten then. It was during the war, and he was home on leave from the First Virginia. Things weren't as bad in Richmond as they got later. We had a big party. The men were all in uniform, and there was dancing. I helped my sister dress for the wedding. She had my mother's white gown. She talked a lot. About what—about what would happen to her. How she had saved herself for the right man, and how wonderful it was going to be, and how it would be wonderful for me when I found the right man. And she talked about what men and women do when they're in love. She had to, because Mother was dead and she was my big sister, and she thought I ought to know."

Laura was silent for a moment. Then she laughed. "So I saved myself for that Comanche buck." Her laugh was bitter, and ruined the peace of the afternoon.

Slocum couldn't think of anything to say.

"And now I'm scared," she said. She rolled over to stare at the rushing stream. Her voice changed, became softer. "When I was learning to ride, whenever I fell off, they made me get back on. They said if I didn't, I would be afraid all my life. John, it's that way now. I don't want to be afraid of men and love, but I am afraid, and it's getting worse; all I can think of is that Comanche, and I don't want to be afraid, I don't—" She looked at Slocum. "Help me."

Slocum felt his manhood hardening. But she was so little, and her voice so like a little girl's! Nineteen, he told himself. Plenty old enough. But—

Memories haunted him from a dead past. Of a time when for boys of his society there were girls you could sleep with and girls you might marry, and they weren't the same girls, ever; and this one was—

This was a girl who had spent years on the plains and had no place to go, just a hope about California, and she couldn't be ruined more than she had been. . . .

"Pretend with me," Laura said. "Show me how it might have been. How it might have been if we'd won the war, and we met afterwards, and we were in love. How it might have been, my first time, if it hadn't been for the war and the Indians." She moved over to lie against him, and put her arms around him. "Help me. Pretend with me. Please."

He turned to her and gently kissed her, his lips barely touching hers, his tongue coming forward to brush her lips, no more than that. It had been a long time since he'd kissed like that. Since before the war. Since then the women had been whores, and none were the kind you kissed, not gently and generally not at all. It was hard to remember what it had been like, before, long before. He could barely recall it. Formal dances. Crinoline skirts, stiff tunics, young men with swords and gold lace and brass buttons, waltzes and formal dances. Another world, a world long dead and gone. He kissed her again.

She moved in his arms, stirring softly, her lips parted in a faint smile. She was trembling.

It might have been this way, Slocum thought. At another time in another world it might have been. He let his fingers gently stroke her arms and shoulders as he touched her lips with his tongue. He felt her response, hesitant and afraid, trying too hard and scared. His fingers strayed gently to her breasts. Softly, he told himself. She's no whore. Not somebody you found in a dance hall. Softly. He felt the young flesh harden at his touch. He continued to stroke her and kiss her, gently, slowly.

She sighed and moved closer to him, pressing herself against him. Her hands went behind his back, but she didn't know what to do with them. Slocum continued to guide her, never doing anything to alarm her. Slow and careful.

His manhood stiffened against her. She stirred and pressed herself harder against him. She felt the pressure against her belly and tensed with fear. His lips moved to her shoulders, and his fingers unbuttoned her blouse. He let his hands stray down to her legs, to stroke her thighs and move upward, not too far. She was like a young filly, wanting friendship, attracted but afraid. He felt the nipples harden beneath his touch, and he brought his lips to her breasts. His darting tongue circled the nipples. She sighed, and his hands moved restlessly across her thighs, upward again.

Her fingers went hesitantly to his cock, pulled away, returned. She explored inside his pants. Her hands were warm, and he felt himself grow harder and harder, steel-hard. She moved against him again. Now her body moved with involuntary motions, hips thrusting forward.

He opened her blouse wider and let his tongue move around her breasts again, downward toward the soft belly, his lips moist, his tongue darting. She began to writhe in pleasure, and he slid her skirt off, his hands stroking upward into the warm tangle of blond hair between her legs. She spread her knees and his fingers slowly touched the soft moistness of her, found the clitoris, moved inside. His fingers opened his pants, and her hand pushed them downward. Slocum kicked them off. Now the two lay naked against each other in the warm afternoon sun.

His tongue and fingers searched her body and she moved. He lifted himself and gently moved between her legs, lowered himself carefully, his fingers opening her warm softness. He let the tip of his cock go in and moved it carefully, slowly, not thrusting home, using only the tip of his iron-hard cock to stroke the stiffened clitoris. He began the ancient rhythm, but slowly, thrusting deeper each time.

She exploded into shouting ecstasy. She lifted her hips against his, pushing herself up, her hands clawing at his buttocks to pull him closer, pull him all the way in. Locked together, they rolled and thrust, faster and faster, and he thrust deeper and deeper, feeling himself fall into her. She shouted again in pleasure. He felt the shuddering waves overtake him, and they moved frantically, desperately, until he exploded into her and they fell exhausted to the blanket.

They lay, drained. She made soft purring sounds. Her hands moved over his body, and she whispered his name. After a long time, he felt himself grow hard within her again, and they coupled once more before falling into exhausted sleep.

"Thank you." He woke to find her sitting beside him. She had made a small fire and had the coffee pot going. "Thank you." She smiled. "It might have been that way. The first time. Now I know how my sister— Thank you, John Slocum."

VII

Later they sat together by the small fire that Slocum thought they could risk. They were camped in a protected draw, and the fire wouldn't be visible from very far away. Even this close to Santa Fe the plains weren't safe.

The night was chilly, and they sat wrapped in a blanket.

"I feel like a bride," Laura said.

Slocum tightened his hold on her waist. He stared into the fire. Bride. The word called up pictures and thoughts he hadn't had for years. Why not? he wondered. Maybe something would work out.

He'd always expected to marry, back before the war changed everything. He wasn't a drifter from any real choice he'd made. There just hadn't been anything else to do. But maybe they could work something out. Go somewhere new, where no one knew either of them, and start a new life. He wouldn't mind working if he had something to work for. He'd seen too many drifters go through life with nothing at all.

Just maybe. "Where will you look for your father?" he asked.

"San Bernardino, California. I have a name to ask for."

"San Bernardino. That's a long way," Slocum said. "And there's been a lot of years. Laura, there's a good chance your father's dead."

"No. We had a letter."

"From him?"

"It had—it had the right words in it," she said. "It wasn't from him, but nobody else could have known what to say."

"All right. It will take a while to get there."

"I know."

"And you still haven't told me his name."

"John, it isn't my secret. Maybe we won't find him. If we do, and if you're still with me—"

Slocum laughed. "You stay smart that way. No point in trusting every drifter you meet."

"It isn't that, and you're not a drifter. But—"

"I know," Slocum said. "I used to know a lot about honor. Haven't had much call for it in the past few years, but I can remember. We'll go look for your father. After all, San Bernardino could be on our way."

She moved closer to him. "Our way?"

"Could be," he said. "We'll see if it works out."

"I like that," she said.

They didn't talk about the future anymore, but they had an understanding. Slocum decided he liked that fine.

They sold the mule in Santa Fe, along with most of Ben Dobbs's outfit. Slocum kept the Spencer buffalo rifle. It had a brass telescope sight and was in excellent condition. "Maybe I can use it to make a living," he said.

They counted up their money. There wasn't a lot to spare. He had to pay extra to the livery man for oats and hay to condition Dorkus; the horse would have to run along behind the stage, and even with no load that would be a strenuous trip.

The livery man offered to buy him, but Slocum wouldn't sell. "Best horse I've had in years," he told Laura. "We'll need him, too." He counted the money again. "Stage comes through in two days. We don't have a lot extra. One hotel room or two?"

"What will we do with the money we save?"

"Buy you a new dress."

She laughed. "Then I guess we'll just have to tell them we're married, won't we? It's better than having them know about"—her voice caught—"about the other—"

"I don't ever want you to talk about that again," Slocum said. He could see that the memory of her two nights with the Comanches was setting her crazy. She brooded on it, and when she did, her eyes glazed over in a frightening way, and she didn't hear when he spoke to her.

He sent her into the general store to buy a traveling dress. When she came out, he almost didn't recognize her. In the yellow frock and bonnet she looked like a woman, not a frightened girl. Her eyes danced with laughter and excitement when they registered as "Mr. and Mrs. C. MacFarlane of Texarkana," and the clerk gave them knowing looks. A couple of elderly female guests whispered loudly about newlyweds as they climbed the stairs to their room.

"I like it," she said when they were inside. "People think we're honeymooners, and I like it."

"I could get used to the idea myself," Slocum said.

Her face lit with pleasure, as it always began to when he said anything about their future. Slocum smiled wryly to himself. He had himself a woman.

A good woman. There were plenty who had to talk about things until they were spoiled, but she didn't do that. She was all right. "That's a right smart outfit you've got on," he told her.

She laughed. A girl's laugh. "Quite a change from when we rode into town."

"There's another outfit I like better."

She smiled. "Yes?"

He took her in his arms. He was about to say that he liked what she wore when he first saw her, but she'd never be able to joke about that. Never. She couldn't even think about it. Slocum wondered if it'd be better if she talked about it, cried about it, but he didn't know.

Don't know a damn thing about ladies, he thought. I should. I grew up around them. But I don't. And I'd best be careful with this one. She's worth holding on to.

He wondered if he'd ever be able to tame himself, go back to being the kind of man he'd been before the war. He'd thought of it once or twice, but he'd never had any reason to do it.

Now maybe I've got one, he thought. Hell, there's only one way to find out.

It was growing dark out when they went downstairs

to eat. They smiled back at the knowing looks from the old ladies in the lobby.

The stage moved south along the Rio Grande to Las Cruces, then turned west and climbed gently. To Slocum it seemed that they were not climbing at all, but one day the driver told him that from here on all rivers flowed into the Pacific. The driver kept the stage moving fast through Apache territory, and was glad to have Slocum and his weapons aboard. They had an army escort through the passes and across the lands of Cochise.

Everyone treated them as newlyweds, and after a while Slocum began to believe it himself. He had plenty of time to think as they came down from the Continental Divide into the Gila Valley and struck west toward Yuma. It was a strange feeling, to be respectable, to be called "Mister" and have people be polite to him, Laura in his bed at night in the stage stops, her quick smile whenever he looked at her, a woman to look out for him and worry about him and see that he was fed and comfortable, to mend his clothes—a woman who needed John Slocum.

It was all worth keeping.

There had to be a way—some way to come up with enough cash to buy a new life. He didn't fancy stealing it. He was sick of having the law after him, of looking back over his shoulder and wondering who might be coming. They were moving far west, a long way from anybody who ever cared about John Slocum. California was just getting settled. There'd be a need for men.

He thought about what he could do. He had a military education, with some engineering training. He had weapons, and a horse, and a couple of hundred dollars somebody owed him. It wasn't a lot, but hell, he told himself, it was a lot more than many a man started with.

When Laura put her head on his shoulder and trustingly went to sleep, Slocum knew he had what he wanted. He'd learned surveying at West Point. Hell, he could work on the railroad. Or partner up with somebody to work a ranch. Or even try some mining. He'd heard about silver strikes in southern California. They hadn't taught a lot about mine engineering at the Point, but he knew some and could learn the rest.

There had to be a lot of ways to make a living, and he'd try them all until he found one. Find a good living and marry this girl and be somebody again.

No more drifting.

Slocum decided he liked that just fine.

VIII

San Bernardino had been settled by Mormons, and the streets were wide and straight. The Mormons had been ordered back to Deseret, and most had obeyed their bishops, so that for a while the town was bigger than its population. There were ranches and farms nearby but not enough to support the town the Mormons had built.

Then the Southern Pacific planned its rail line between Los Angeles and the rest of the world. One branch would go up from the coastal plains to the high desert through Cajon Pass, another southeast to Yuma. San Bernardino was a natural place for the division repair facilities and track-construction headquarters. Surveyors laid out the routes. Loggers came to fell timber for cross ties. The SP began to lay track, and suddenly the town began to boom. The streets were crowded with Irish and Chinese workers just coming in, none of them wanted by the ranchers and farmers who'd lived there for years.

Slocum and Laura found a hotel room in the old town where railroad workers were not allowed. Signs along the main east-west road said NO IRISH OR CHINESE NORTH OF HERE, and deputy sheriffs patrolled the deadline to enforce it.

After sundown it was possible to breathe. They went for a stroll in their "safe" part of town. A bearded man in a bowler hat was arguing with one of the deputy sheriffs who did not want his wagon across the deadline. Slocum stared at the old man.

"God damn," John said softly.

Laura looked a question at him, puzzled by the unusual profanity.

"That's Abraham Sheffield," Slocum said. "Remember him?"

Laura gasped. "Yes. He sold needles, and Dresden thimbles. Once, he brought me a doll from France."

Slocum nodded. "My father bought me marbles. From Bohemia. And Chinese firecrackers. And that deputy's treating him like a nigger."

"Don't make trouble, John. Mr. Sheffield can take care of himself."

Which was true enough. Before Slocum could step forward, Mr. Sheffield convinced the deputy that he, too, was a white man. The deputy pocketed the dollar and walked away. Slocum started to go forward to speak to Sheffield, but Laura pulled him back. She'd kept her face turned away from Sheffield.

Doesn't want to be recognized, Slocum thought. And she's right: we don't want to call attention to our past, not if we're going to live out here. But damn it, that old man was our friend, a long time ago. . . .

"Unfriendly place," Slocum said.

"We won't be here long." Laura gave him a sidewise glance. "We've walked and ridden clear across the country, and now we're letting a good hotel room go to waste. . . ."

Slocum grinned. "Right."

As they walked back to the hotel, a huge, beefy man backed out of a barroom door still talking to someone inside. Turning abruptly, he plowed into Laura. She gasped and staggered back. The red-faced man studied her as he patted his wallet pocket. Laura flushed under his leisurely inspection.

"There's a special god who protects fools and drunkards," Slocum said. "But some days he's awfully busy."

The man took in Slocum's stance, the holstered Colt, and the Bowie knife. He gave Laura another casually undressing stare before tipping his hat. "Sorry, ma'am." He stepped back into the taproom.

"That man wasn't drunk," Laura said as they went up to their room.

"Perhaps he'll not be a fool, either."

"Couldn't you have let it pass?"

"You wouldn't have been able to walk a block in this town without feeling a man's hand on you."

Laura sighed. "I suppose you're right." Then she brightened. "But it doesn't have to spoil our afternoon."

Slocum grinned. They went up to their room and put the bed to proper use. Afterward, staring at the Chinese-papered ceiling, she mused, "Now I have to find Henry Marshall."

"There's something deficient about me?"

Laura bent to kiss his deficiency, and Slocum felt himself rise to the occasion. "I don't even know if Henry Marshall is alive," she murmered, while doing something that made Slocum very aware that he was. "Ooohh, that's nice. But Henry Marshall's the name Cracker told me to look for."

"Right now?"

"Ooooh nooo. Not yet!"

Later Slocum lay smoking a cheroot. He had never pressed her for information. He figured Laura would tell him when she was ready, and he was in no hurry.

She opened the windows and went out to the small balcony that adjoined their room. "It's a lovely place," she said.

Slocum came out to join her. "Sure is. Too bad everybody's so plumb hateful."

"They can't all be," she said. "And look."

High mountains rose abruptly from the plains where the town lay. They thrust upward into the northern sky, high peaks covered with trees, pierced by canyons with streams. The whole northern skyline was filled with mountains so close that you could be in them in a day's walk. Some had snow even in midsummer.

From time to time there were the sounds of nitro as the railroad men blasted into the foothills, clearing the way for the tracks that would go north through the Mojave Desert and on to San Francisco.

On the streets below there was an air of expectancy; this part of San Bernardino was filled with people who had dreams and hope and work to do.

"Your father live here?" Slocum asked.

"I don't know," Laura said. "I never heard of the place until Cracker told me we were coming here."

"He give any idea how to find this Henry Marshall?"

"No."

"Guess I'll just have to ask around. You get unpacked, and I'll go looking. We don't have enough money to stay here long. I can probably find work with the railroad, but it'd be best if we find your father pretty quick, before we run out of cash. Any reason to keep it secret that we're loookking for Henry Marshall?"

"I don't think so," Laura said. "But I don't know. Cracker said that Marshall was expecting him."

Slocum shrugged. "So I tell people that Laura MacFarlane wants to talk to Henry Marshall. Who do I say I am?" They were registered at the hotel under the name of MacFarlane. "I sure don't look like Cracker."

And that's a blessing, Slocum thought, as he remembered that eyeless remnant of a man.

A week later they were almost out of money, and Slocum thought he'd better do something about it. The Arrowhead Hotel seemed to be where all the important locals hung out. The poker game in its elegant saloon was peopled with businessmen, land owners, city councilmen, even a county commissioner. Slocum struck up a conversation with a rancher whose accent placed him from Carolina, and soon he was invited to join the game.

The game was played for higher stakes than Slocum could afford, and Slocum had to be careful. He also had to buy a round of drinks, which put him down further. But everyone was friendly, and even if he won no money, he was lucky to get to meet some of the more powerful men of the community; if he and Laura settled here, these people would be worth knowing. Slocum played on.

One of the players was a deputy sheriff. After two hours of play, the sheriff came in to join the game. The deputy stood. "Guess it's time to make rounds," he said. "Everyone excuse me."

The sheriff was a huge, horse killer of a man. He

wasn't so much fat, just big. His face was raw beef from a sun that scorched but could not tan him. "Les Bigelow," he announced as he sat down. He looked curiously at Slocum. "Do I know you?"

"John Slocum." Slocum wondered if the beefy sheriff was pretending not to remember how close he had come to jostling his last woman.

"New in town." The sheriff didn't make it a question. "Thinking about staying?"

"Possibly."

The sheriff glanced inquiringly at Commissioner Davis, then turned back to Slocum. "You'll like it here. Place is growing. Well, gentlemen, I can't stay long. Shall we play?"

John had seen uglier, more pig-eyed men, but there was something about Sheriff Bigelow that put him off. The sheriff often smiled, but only with the bottom half of his face. The tiny blue eyes remained cold and watchful.

Bigelow bought into the game for only five dollars' worth of chips, grinning as he did. "Damn silly ordinance," he said, referring to a local law against there being money on the table. "But I gotta enforce it."

Slocum had played cautiously, not daring to back his big hands, slowly building his fifty dollars into eighty. Now there was a sudden *feel* around the table. Up to now the men at the table had played well or poorly as God had endowed them, and he had never caught any hint of bottom-dealing or collusion among the others; but now invisible waves of something passed around the table.

Slocum had sensed this sort of thing before. When he passed through strange territory, it usually meant the local boys were ganging up to trim the stranger. Slocum could not afford a lesson just now. Every instinct told him to toss in his cards and call it a night.

But these men had never played that way, and they were looking at the sheriff, not at Slocum. While John thought about that, the sheriff tossed in a dollar to open. John looked at his hand. Three tens. Much too good a hand to throw in. Slocum put in his dollar.

Everyone at the table stayed in. That didn't make

sense. They couldn't all have that good a hand. And none of them drew cards, no one except Slocum. He took two, and didn't improve.

Damn it, he thought, there is something *very* wrong here.

The sheriff tossed in four dollars, everything he had bought in for. One by one the others threw in dollar chips. Then they threw down their hands. The sheriff began raking in the pot.

"I'm still playing," Slocum said.

The sheriff looked genuinely puzzled. "You say something?"

"Only that I'm still playing." Slocum tossed in his four dollars. Had this beefy bastard's eyes been so busy undressing Laura that he actually could not remember Slocum?

The sheriff scooped Slocum's chips up along with the rest of the pot.

"May I see your hand, please?" Slocum's polite voice brought the sheriff's grasping hand to a halt. He glared at Slocum and noticed for the first time that John held his cards fanned in his left hand; his right was not on the table.

"You tryin' to accuse me of something?" the sheriff demanded.

"Surely not," Commissioner Davis said. "Mr. Slocum, I don't think you understand."

"I merely ask that the game be played by the customary rules," Slocum said. "Show your cards, please. The hand has been called."

He cursed himself for a fool even as he spoke. Now that it was too late to back down, John understood what was happening. The sheriff used this game —and probably all the others in town—to collect tribute from a town totally under his control. The solid citizens like Davis had needed someone to keep the Irish and the Chinese in their place. Too late they'd discovered the inevitable: that a man who does nothing to protect others will someday find no one to protect him. And they still needed this bully to keep the riffraff out of their exclusive corner of creation.

Understanding the situation didn't do anything for

Slocum's problem. Why the hell hadn't he let the man take his dollar and be done with it?

"We play by different rules here," the sheriff growled.

"I've noticed that," Slocum said icily. Still not moving he added, "But you put up signs to warn the Irish and the Chinese. It would only be common courtesy to do the same for a white man."

"What do you mean by that?"

"Only that I'll see your cards, or the pot remains in play."

Commissioner Davis frowned and left the table. So did the rancher who'd invited Slocum into the game.

"It'll cost you another ten dollars to see my hand," the sheriff said. His voice was still carefully controlled.

"Very well," Slocum said. "Chips only, please. Local ordinances forbid money . . ."

The sheriff almost laughed. Then he took a ten-dollar chip from his vest pocket and tossed it onto the table.

Slocum wondered if his brains had all turned to grits. The sheriff played here. He obviously didn't cash in each time he left.

"And another ten," the big man said. His lip curled into a contemptuous smile. "Had enough?"

"No. And twenty more," Slocum said. He sat unmoving, his right hand still out of sight, his eyes on the sheriff's, waiting for the flick of eyebrow and widening of eye that would give him a split second's warning.

The sheriff stared back. Finally he dropped his cards on the table. "I'll be seeing you again," he said. "Good night, Mr. Slocum."

"Good night, Sheriff." He waited until the big man went out the door before looking around. The other players were at the bar, pointedly not looking in Slocum's direction. John made his cautious way back to the hotel, feeling eyes on his back all the way, but nothing happened. The sheriff, he supposed, would go in for more subtle methods. After all, California was a state, and the railroads were trying to get people to settle here. The powerful men in Sacramento wouldn't put up with a local sheriff who made California sound like a lawless territory.

He cursed himself as he walked. He'd been hoping to settle here. Now he'd have to watch his back constantly, and he'd sure not be invited back into that game, which was too bad, because he'd made some money there and could have made more.

Of course, there'd be penny-ante games south of the deadline, but he didn't want to go there. Thinking like a gentleman he told himself, and managed a dry laugh. But it was true.

If he'd managed to control himself, to let that brutish bandit of a sheriff have his dollar's worth of tribute, Slocum could have tried the railroad offices near city hall. There might be an opening for an engineer or surveyor. It could have done for a while, until he thought of something else Everyone he met told him how the country was opening up, growing, lots of opportunities. There'd been two other Southerners at the Arrowhead game table, and both had come out here with nothing and now had spreads of their own. They'd tightened their lips when the sheriff sat down, but they put in their money without saying anything —and they sure didn't admire John Slocum for making a scene, either.

Well, maybe, Slocum told himself. Maybe there's something to playing straight, and hell, paying off the sheriff in a poker game's no worse than taxes. He imagined himself as a rancher, married to Laura, with kids running around the place. It would be dull, but there was a lot going for the idea. If he could make peace with the sheriff.

Buy the man a drink, offer to cut cards for money, and pointedly lose without looking at the cards. That would show Sheriff Bigelow that John Slocum knew both sides of the score, that he would play by the rules but wasn't *forced* to. Hell, John thought, I could come out better than if I'd just paid without trouble. *But would he demand Laura as the next installment?* Slocum was certain the town madams paid their tribute without using cash. But it was unlikely that the city fathers would put up with a sheriff who couldn't leave their wives alone. The sheriff would have to make compromises. Once Slocum was known as a man who'd play the game, he and Laura would be left alone.

But first they had to find Laura's father. Slocum wasn't sure the man was alive. They had nothing to go on, only the name Henry Marshall, and Laura still wouldn't tell him her father's real name.

Another week, he thought, and we'll forget it. I'll take her down to the courthouse and marry her, and we'll get started on building a new life. He'd outbluffed the sheriff twice. With luck he wouldn't have to do it again.

The sheriff's office was near the railroad headquarters. Before Slocum could go into the Southern Pacific offices, he saw Jim Cavanaugh coming out of the sheriff's door.

"Slocum," Cavanaugh said. "Glad to see you again. See you got here."

"Sure. What brings you here?" Slocum asked.

Cavanaugh shrugged. "Heard they made some strikes up in the Mojave. Got my mining equipment to sell. Always wondered what happened with that girl. You bring her here?"

"Yeah," Slocum said.

"Pretty girl. She all right?"

Slocum nodded. "I guess we'll be getting married."

"Good. Got to invite me to the wedding," Cavanaugh said.

"Reckon you've earned that." And more, Slocum thought. Cavanaugh's last shot in the fight at the Comanche camp made the score uneven. Slocum owed Cavanaugh one.

"So what are you doing?" Cavanaugh asked.

"Looking for work. Thought I'd try the Southern Pacific. Hear they're looking for men."

"I expect they are. Hey, let me buy you a drink." Cavanaugh walked them toward the Silver Dollar saloon. Before they got there, a young deputy came out of the sheriff's office and ran toward them.

"Mr. Cavanaugh," the deputy called. "Message for you." Cavanaugh excused himself and walked toward the deputy. They talked for a few moments; then Cavanaugh came back to Slocum.

"Looks like that drink will have to wait," Cavanaugh said. "Man I've been looking for is in town. Hey, when you talk to the Southern Pacific, give my name and ask for Hennessey. He's the district superintendent, and he owes me. Can't hurt to talk to him."

"Okay. Thanks," Slocum said. He watched Cavanaugh hurry away, then went to the SP offices. Hennessey wasn't there, nor was the hiring boss, so Slocum went back to the hotel.

When he reached the room, Laura was gone.

The clerk looked smugly at Slocum. "I really can't tell you," he said. "She checked out an hour ago, and there is no forwarding address."

"Who paid the bill?" Slocum demanded.

"The two gentlemen who came for her."

"And who the hell were they?"

The clerk shrugged. His faint smile was maddening.

Slocum nodded. His hand went under his coat. "If I draw this, you're going to be missing your kneecaps," he said. "Maybe you'd rather tell me what happened before I do that. Please."

The clerk glanced around the empty lobby. The smile vanished. "Look, I don't know . . . Wait! Don't do that!" Small beads of sweat formed on his forehead. "I don't know the gentlemen. I understand they work at the Cross Seven. That's a ranch in the high country. Over the mountains, near Summit. It's a timber ranch."

"Who owns it?"

"Mr.—he calls himself 'Misyoor'—Giraud. Frenchman. He doesn't get to town much. The two gentlemen who came for Mrs. MacFarlane are Americans. Southerners, I think. One is the ranch manager—Captain Crowley. They seemed to know Mrs. MacFarlane. They were in a great hurry to leave."

"I owe anything on the bill?"

"No, sir. The gentlemen paid it."

"And no messages for me?"

"No, sir."

"Thanks." Slocum went up to his room to pack.

Just what the hell do I do now? he wondered. For damned sure he couldn't ask the sheriff for help.

IX

The trail into and over the San Bernardino Mountains was steep and not well marked. Worse, Slocum wasn't sure where he was going. One of his poker acquaintances knew of the Cross Seven but had never been there. There were a dozen timber ranches in the forests sloping down to the Mojave Desert; soon there would be more. The Southern Pacific was going to need a lot of cross ties.

His acquaintance had met Monsieur Giraud only once. Like Slocum, Giraud had been an officer in the Emperor Maximilian's army before Napoleon III withdrew the Legion and left Maximilian to his fate. John couldn't remember him, but that wasn't surprising. The Legion regulars hadn't cared for mercenary officers, even though most had seen more combat in the Civil War than the legionnaires had in all of France's colonial adventures.

No one knew him well, because Giraud didn't welcome visitors. The poker player told Slocum where he thought the ranch would be, but he wasn't sure.

"Fool's errand," Slocum told his mount. But he couldn't stay in town now. He had got to his poker-playing friend only a short jump ahead of the news. There would be no place in this or any other town for a man whose wife had been taken away and who hadn't the gumption to go get her back. And he sure as hell didn't expect any help from the sheriff!

Dorkus nickered in answer, and continued to strain up the steep sloping trail through the pine forest.

"Did she go, or did they take her? And why no word for me? Nothing. Why? And what the hell does she have to do with Maximilian and the Foreign Legion?" John laughed at himself. He wasn't going to get an answer from Dorkus, and there wasn't anyone else to ask.

An hour later there was, but he wasn't asking.

A dozen horsemen in small, flat-crowned sombreros rode from a side trail. They called to each other in Spanish, and one blocked Slocum's way.

"Good afternoon, *señor,*" the leader said. He was a big man with a heavy black walrus mustache. He wore fancy Mexican boots and clothing and a sombrero with tiny gold beads dangling from the brim.

Slocum kept his hand near his pistol. No one had drawn on him yet. With a dozen to face he hadn't much hope of fighting them anyway. *"Buenas tardes,"* Slocum answered.

"And where are you going on such a fine day?"

Slocum decided it couldn't hurt to be polite. Probably wouldn't help either. "Mojave," he said.

"A dry place. A man could be killed there," the leader said. "Permit me. I am Tiburcio Vásquez."

Slocum had heard of Vásquez. A stage robber who had once taken over an entire town and stolen every cent in it, he was now rumored to have stolen hundreds of horses and cattle that he kept in a hidden canyon in the mountains. The story was that Vásquez wouldn't rob poor Mexicans, but he considered everyone else from San Francisco to San Diego a fair prize. The California Rangers had been after him for years, but they'd never caught him.

"No, the Mojave is not a healthy place," Vásquez said. "It would be a shame to allow you to go there. You might die of thirst. And we need another horse. Do not put your hand to your pistol, *señor*. You would not live to draw it."

There were two distinct clicks behind Slocum—two pistols cocked and aimed at him.

"As you must know, I seldom kill anyone," Vásquez said. "There is no need." He stood in his saddle and bowed elaborately. "Now, if you will do me the favor of dismounting. Thank you. And the pistol. Please remove the belt. And of course what you have in your pockets. . . ."

One of the bandits took the reins and led Slocum's

horse away. Another dismounted and picked up his pistol and wallet from the ground.

"Un millón de gracias," Vásquez said.

"You may as well shoot me," Slocum said. "Leave me in the mountains with no horse and no gun. You might as well murder me now and get it over with."

Vásquez stroked his thick mustache. "That is true," he said. He looked thoughtful for a moment, then laughed. "Juan. Your spare pistol."

One of the bandits cross-drew a pistol from his left side. He grasped it carefully in both fists and aimed it at Slocum. John could see the whitening of a brown finger as the bandit took up slack in the trigger. He saw the tallow plugs in the cylinder and knew the weapon was loaded. At the last possible instant the bandit shifted his aim and the ball whizzed past Slocum's ear.

John stood rigid, waiting for the smoke to clear. "So now we know it shoots," he snapped. "Now are you going to give it to me, or must we continue with barbaric games?"

Juan's face darkened as the other bandits laughed. His finger whitened again, and this time Slocum knew he was not planning on any last-minute change of aim.

"¡Basta!" Vásquez ordered. "Juan, I give you the gelding. Is that not fair—a new horse for an old pistol?"

Juan would obviously have been happier if the exchange had been managed without tattering his dignity, but he handed the pistol to Vásquez. The bandit leader took the cylinder out and dropped the weapon on the ground. "I will leave the other parts and the powder and balls up the trail," he said. "You will find them easily. I regret that this is not the best we have but it is what we can give. It failed its last owner only once." He laughed. "That is why Hernando no longer needs a pistol. *Vámanos, muchachos.*" He wheeled and rode away. The others followed.

Slocum picked up the discarded pistol. It had a large dent near the end of the barrel. There were smears of lead. A shot had struck the pistol there,

John concluded. Which was why it had failed, and probably why Hernando's pistol was carried as a spare by a man named Juan.

He followed the outlaws until he found the cylinder. There was a good powder flask, a leather bag with two dozen balls for the pistol, and a small leather bag of grease. "Bastard left me everything I need," John muttered. He loaded and assembled the weapon, then took careful aim at a mark on a nearby tree and fired. The ball struck high and to the right. The weapon was badly bent, and the sights were useless.

He made camp for the night, building a fire by picking a strip of his shirt tail into lint for tinder, then striking a spark from the butt of the pistol on a flint rock. The only good thing he could see about the situation was that there was plenty of flint.

When dawn came, he had to make up his mind. He could follow Vásquez, but that wasn't likely to work. If Vásquez were in the habit of leaving a trail, the rangers would have caught him long ago—and what could Slocum do if he did catch up to the outlaws?

He could go back to San Bernardino and try to get help. That didn't seem too useful, either. Vásquez was famous. Everyone knew he was holed up somewhere in these mountains. If they knew where, they'd have gone in and hanged him a long time ago.

He began the long climb toward the summit. He'd set out to find Laura and the Cross Seven, and that still seemed the best thing to do.

There was plenty of water, and he could build a fire. The pistol was no damned good, but he might be able to shoot a squirrel if one got close enough and held still.

At least, he told himself, I still have cavalry boots. A lot of men bought themselves boots that were no damned good for walking.

It wasn't much consolation.

About noon he realized he wasn't alone. There was someone following him. Someone damned good. Slocum never saw anyone, and he wasn't really sure there was anyone there for another hour; then an arrow flashed past his head.

He turned quickly, in time to see a grinning Indian face. Slocum snapped a shot at it.

The Indian was moving fast, so fast that Slocum had no chance to see him. The only thing he was sure of was the grin, a wide grin of sheer amusement. At that range, and shooting so quickly, Slocum had no real chance of a hit even with good sights. With this pistol it was hopeless. He had no idea where the ball went. The Indian seemed to be laughing as he vanished behind a tree.

The arrow had missed by a foot and embedded itself in a tree. It had a flint head held on by thin leather wrappings. It meant nothing to Slocum. He wasn't familiar with the local tribes. No one had warned him of Indians in the mountains. Bandits, grizzly bears, and rattlesnakes; those he'd been told to worry about, but not Indians. Slocum couldn't remember hearing about any Indian wars in southern California.

So this had to be a bandit. An Indian turned bandit. "And what the hell do you want from me?" Slocum said aloud. "Vásquez got everything already." He laughed, but it wasn't really all that funny. Vásquez had left him his clothes and boots. Men had died to save less. Given this flinty terrain, the boots were worth his life.

The Indian wasn't around. Slocum was sure of that. He heard nothing and saw nothing. Still, he had a feeling of being watched, and though that wasn't always reliable, it often had been when he was in the army.

An hour went by; then suddenly there was a shout, and the sound of snarls and growls in the scrub forest above him. Someone yelled a loud war cry. There were more growls and snarls and the sound of brush being trampled.

Suddenly an Indian burst from the bushes about twenty yards ahead of John and fifty yards higher up the slope. The man scrambled downhill, yelling. He caught sight of Slocum, slowed for a moment, then yelled again and went on running downhill, stumbling in the loose turf, scrambling up and running for his life.

Behind him bounded a very large bear. It was brown, with gray tips at the fur. John Slocum had never seen a grizzly bear, but he had heard of them. "Mean as hell," he'd been told. "Only damn thing I know of that'll attack a man as often as not. Mean bastards."

This one was ten yards behind the Indian, and gaining.

Slocum drew his pistol. Then he hesitated. What should he shoot? The Indian? From the dull flannel shirt the man wore, this was the same Indian who'd fired an arrow at him earlier.

Or shoot at the bear?

Or do nothing, and let the bear take care of the Indian? The bear wasn't threatening John Slocum.

The Indian ran past. John remembered the grin the last time he'd seen the man's face. Another grin much like it was there now. Like a bitch dog caught eating shit.

Slocum raised the weapon and aimed at the Indian. The man yelled, glanced behind, and continued to run.

"Aw, hell," Slocum said. He shifted his aim, held low, tracked his target for a moment, and fired. The Indian dropped to the ground and lay still. Slocum fired again. The grizzly collapsed and slid and rolled downward until it lay near the Indian.

Slocum walked over cautiously. The bear was motionless, but Slocum held the pistol near its head and shot once more, just to be sure. Then he looked at the fallen man. "It's dead," he said.

"Good thing, walking man," the Indian shouted. "Good thing. You skin him or me?"

Slocum examined his prize. When the Indian started to get up, John held the pistol on him. With a shrug the Indian lay down again. "Somebody skin him," he said.

He was an old man. Slocum couldn't tell how old.

The teeth were yellow and worn down nearly to the gums. The skin of his face and hands had wrinkled and cracked. He wore faded brown pants and an old blue flannel shirt and a leather headband embedded with tiny beads around hair that was startlingly black for someone that old. The voice sounded old, too, high and strong but with an involuntary quaver.

"You skin him, I cook him," the Indian said. He looked at Slocum's face and at the leveled pistol. "Okay, I skin him and I cook him, too. Okay?"

Slocum began to laugh. "Who the hell are you?" he demanded.

"White men call me Mojave Joe, you bet," the Indian said. "You never say my real name. So old I forget my real name. Mojave Joe good enough." He eyed Slocum warily. "Why not skin him?" he demanded. "You eat nothing last night. I eat nothing for two days. Big bear there. Enough for both. Eat good."

"You watched me last night?" Slocum asked.

"Sure I watch. Watch all day, too. You bet."

"Why did you shoot at me?"

Mojave Joe laughed. "Not shoot at you."

"The hell you didn't. Look at this—"

"You keep arrow. Good. Arrows hard to get. That good arrow. If I shoot that arrow at you, I hit you. You bet."

"If you didn't shoot at me, what the hell were you doing?"

"Have fun. White man in forest. No food. No horse. Pistol, no rifle. Not much chance have fun with white men. You bet." The old man sighed. "One time got Yuma wife. Warden man pay me catch man run away prison. Lots fun catch white man then. You bet!"

Slocum couldn't make anything out of that. "What happened to the bow? Oh, hell, get up."

"Sure get up. Thank you. You bet. Bow up there." He pointed up the hill. "Look for good place to hide, watch you come along trail. Find good place. Find place too good. Find place good enough anything to hide. Bear hide there."

That was too much. Slocum threw his head back and roared with laughter.

Slocum retrieved the bow while Mojave Joe busied himself skinning the bear. It was a short, sturdy weapon, quite unlike the Indian bows Slocum had seen on the Texas plains. This one was polished wood, with curves that made it seem very graceful. It lay just where Joe had said it would.

Slocum brought it down and thoughtfully handed it to Mojave Joe. "Shoot it," he ordered. "That tree down there." He pointed to a small pine forty yards away. "There's a white spot on it. Shoot that."

"Don't know. Long shot."

"You better hit it," Slocum said. "You hit it, you prove you didn't try to hit me."

"Okay," Joe said. He nocked an arrow.

"Make damn sure you aim at that tree," Slocum said. "You turn around and I shoot."

Mojave Joe laughed, then drew the arrow back and let fly in a single smooth motion. The arrow stuck in the tree a foot from the mark.

"Pretty good," Slocum said. "So maybe you weren't trying to shoot me."

"You bet," Mojave Joe said. He reached into the animal's opened belly and drew out the liver. He cut off a slice and popped it into his mouth. "You want?"

"Want cooked," Slocum said. "Hell, I'm beginning to talk like you."

"I talk plenty good. Talk Mojave, talk Yuma, talk Apache. Talk Spanish. Learn Spanish in mission. Now new mission. Say Spanish mission no good; Spanish got sick god. New god talk English. I learn that, too. You bet. You want cooked, got have fire." He looked at Slocum and laughed. "Okay, I get wood. White man never want to work."

Mojave Joe was a hundred years old, or claimed to be. Slocum had no way of knowing, but he doubted if the Indian was more than sixty. Joe seemed strong and limber even for that age.

"Strong? Mojave Joe always strong," Joe said. "Run across desert, no water; run across in one day, two day. White man take wagon and mules and water and take many days." He held up all ten fingers several times.

"You know the desert pretty good?" Slocum asked. He lay back, relaxed but wary, keeping his right hand free and near the pistol in his belt.

"Know desert. Know mountains. Know everything around here. Been here a hundred years. You bet."

"Know where the Cross Seven ranch is?"

"Sure. Cross Seven. Men talk funny. Talk a lot. Not talk English much. No talk Spanish much. Other talk."

"Where is the Cross Seven?"

"Over top." Mojave Joe waved toward the northwest. "Three days' walk for white man. Day, two days for Mojave Joe. Not far. I show you. You bet. Mojave Joe know every damn place. You bet."

"Every place. Know where Vásquez is camped?"

Mojave Joe laughed loudly. "I know. You bet. You want go see Vásquez?"

"I'd sure like to get my horse back."

Joe laughed again. "We go. Steal back horse. Why not? I take you. I watch you get killed. You bet."

X

"We'll see about that," Slocum said, and grunted. "But, given any choice in the matter, I'd sooner someone else died."

"Ah?" Mojave Joe's knowledge of English syntax was not profound.

Slocum did not elaborate. Instead he whittled a sapling and cut a thin strip of loin, which he twined around it. While he sat with the stick over the tiny fire, waiting to see what unsalted bear would taste like, Mojave Joe finished off a few more bites of raw liver sprinkled with gall, then got a stick of his own. The old Indian removed a yard of upper intestine and passed it through his fingers to squeeze out most of the semidigested food, then wrapped the gut as Slocum had his loin. After it had sizzled and sputtered for thirty seconds, Joe unwrapped one end and bit off a piece. His seamed face was suddenly a century older with disgust.

"Goddamn bear eat skunk!" he muttered as he threw the stick into the fire.

Hastily, Slocum removed his half-cooked back bacon from the greasy smudge that arose. He had not realized bear could be so stringy. If the loin was like this, what were the tough parts like?

"Why you no eat good?" Joe asked as he delved into the carcass for a kidney. "You eat dog food."

"Chacun à son goût," Slocum explained.

"You talk like them feller Cross Seven."

That confirmed one thing. Mojave Joe had actually been to the Cross Seven.

Mojave Joe ignored him as he chipped away at the grizzly's skull with a shard of flint. Finally he had the brain pan open. "You like?"

There was a time when Slocum had been partial to

calves' brains broiled, buttered, even in omelets. But their crumbly consistency demanded a skillet. He discovered that raw grizzly brains, if not exactly tasty, were at least less tough than other parts of this stringy predator.

Slocum and Mojave Joe belched at the same moment. They grinned and were sleepy. Suddenly it was hours later, the sun already disappearing in the western slopes, and Joe was shaking him. Slocum wondered whatever had happened to his fine-honed sense of self-preservation.

"You want see Vásquez?"

"Agreed. But not reciprocally."

"You say?"

"I'd like to see him but I'd prefer that Señor Vásquez not see me."

"I see."

"Let us pray he and his minions do not."

"Le's go."

Slocum got to his feet and was abruptly reminded of how far he had walked in cavalry boots. It was not his accustomed form of exercise. He managed to suppress a groan. They finished climbing the ridge, and he discovered a whole new set of aches and strains as Joe, pigeon-toed, made his way down the other side of the mountain. Slocum was having difficulty breathing, but he would not let himself be outwalked by this indestructible eater of intestines.

He clenched his teeth and breathed through them, fighting not to let the wrinkled old Indian know how close he was to collapse. They dog-trotted another mile, and Slocum could not imagine where his body could have held all that moisture. But still he sprayed sweat from every pore. His throat ached. Jesus! He would sell his immortal soul for a tall glass of branch and bourbon, a rocking chair. He was preparing to swallow his pride and ask the old man to slow down when finally Joe turned in gathering darkness and put finger to lips.

"You make lotta noise," the old man said.

Slocum struggled to halt without collapsing. "Somebody close?" he managed.

"You bet. Lotsa somebody."

"Who?"

"Who you come see?"

Slocum goggled. "Vásquez?"

"Why you make so goddamn much noise?"

From the glint of amusement in the old man's eye Slocum knew his condition was no secret. "On a horse I wouldn't," he said.

"You be quiet. Now we go slow."

By the time they reached the rimrock, Slocum's breathing had returned nearly to normal, though he was still drenched in sweat. The moon had risen, and the steep-walled meadow and creek below them were only half in shadow. Near a bend in the creek, fires glinted before several ramadas and one more permanent structure with walls as well as roof. Someone was playing a guitar and singing in a mournful, nasal voice.

"Okay?" Mojave Joe asked. "You see Tiburcio Vásquez. Now we go?"

"No."

"You crazy sumbitch. Be quiet. You think we 'lone up here?"

Slocum guessed it would be asking too much for a man who had evaded the law this many years not to have pickets posted about his stronghold. "But we must be fairly alone," he said. "You're talking."

"Be quiet."

Slocum deemed it expedient to obey. In the darkness he could hear a horse blowing. An instant later he heard the creak of leather and jingle of bit. Somebody was riding toward them.

As Slocum scooted back from the edge of the rimrock, a pebble came loose and went rattledebang down a hundred yards of nearly perpendicular slope. Mojave Joe emitted the faintest suggestion of a groan and was abruptly missing—gone off into darkness back under the trees away from the rimrock edge.

Slocum squinted. He still could not see the horse or its rider, but if he were to stand, they would certainly see him out here on the bald rock edge. He began easing back toward the timber.

"*¿Qué hubo?*" somebody called from the camp.

Slocum's hand found another shard of loose rock. He wished most devoutly that he had never dislodged that first one, but it was too late to undo history. He threw the rock as far into the meadow below as he could manage without standing.

"Cabrón Juan sigue enojado." Slocum could hear the words clearly a hundred yards below him. Another voice agreed that that cuckold of a Juan was still angry but that was no reason for him to take it out on his own comrades and maybe they ought to go up there and throw the *hijo de la rechingada* over the edge.

Slocum felt a sudden thrill of recognition. He had already met one Juan today. He glanced skyward and directed his prayer in the same direction. Let it be the same Juan, he willed.

An instant later he recognized both the bandit and the gelding. It was Dorkus.

"For this relief, much thanks," he muttered. Dorkus's ears angled forward, which was not lost on his rider. Rifle at ready, the bandit rode Slocum's horse carefully, at a slow walk, through patches of moonlight and darkness. Slocum's prayer had been answered. Why, he wondered, oh, why hadn't he thought to include a request for a little more cover, his Bowie knife, some high ground, an overhanging tree?

Man and horse were almost on top of him when abruptly there was a sound somewhere behind. Juan spurred Dorkus in a quick turn, but all was silence. Slocum had almost forgotten Mojave Joe. Abruptly he realized the old Indian had not forgotten him. He must have tossed that rock.

Juan dithered in a moment of indecision.

Slocum felt about blindly, wishing he'd kept the second rock instead of flinging it over the rimrock. He could find nothing heavy enough to serve his purpose. The gelding pirouetted again, smelling Slocum. Juan sawed at the bridle in a most unhorsemanlike fashion until the beast gave up.

A minute passed. Slocum would have been willing to swear it was an hour, but he had been mindlessly counting the pounding in his ears. Even in the tenseness of the moment it had not thundered more than ninety times as he lay within five feet of man and horse. He was in plain sight, but his dirty, travel-stained clothes were invisible against the rock. As long as he kept his face down and didn't move . . .

A snake rattled.

The horse heard it, too. Dorkus flinched, causing Juan to lose a stirrup momentarily. As the man's foot stabbed blindly, Slocum knew he would not be offered a second chance. He stood quickly, grabbed the bandit's knee just above the boot, and hauled mightily.

Juan gave a wild shriek of alarm as he sailed from the saddle. Already his knife was half drawn. Slocum had nothing. Using the momentum of Juan's fall from the horse, he boosted him overhead, spinning and struggling to keep him off balance. Finally the knife clattered on rock. Somewhere in the darkness the snake was still rattling. Slocum threw the slightly built bandit as far as he could and prayed he could reach the knife first. As it turned out, he had plenty of time.

Juan screamed and howled the entire hundred near-vertical yards down the face of the rimrock. Slocum hadn't planned it that way, but—what the hell? Everybody had to die somehow. He caught Dorkus's reins. Abruptly Mojave Joe appeared out of the darkness. "Le's go!" he urged.

Slocum swung up into the saddle and held out a hand for Joe to mount pillion. The ancient Indian was up in a flash. "Le's go!" he repeated. "Goddamn, le's go!"

But Slocum abruptly realized that he was still not quite ready to go. The gelding stood a scant couple of yards from the edge of the rimrock, half silhouetted in moonlight. He urged the beast until they were in the shadow of a ponderosa. "Tiburcio Vásquez!" he hailed. "Don Tiburcio, for the kindness my eternal gratitude. But a man does what he must and I need my horse. Don Tiburcio, my gelding divorces thee." This last was a pun on *Tiburcio* and *divorcio,* which were pronounced almost the same in border Spanish.

"Le's go!"

"All right." Slocum turned his heels inward, then realized he was not wearing spurs. But Dorkus understood his intent and trotted off into the darkness.

"No this way! They get us!"

"But the entrance is at the other end," Slocum protested. "Isn't this a box canyon?"

"You crazy sumbitch! Think Vásquez stupid? He got trail both ways. Nobody catch Vásquez. He sure gon' catch you."

"Now he tells me," Slocum muttered. Dorkus had found some kind of a trail and was breaking into a gallop.

"You crazy sumbitch!" Mojave Joe howled.

Slocum was inclined to agree. There was nothing funny about it.

Why were they both laughing?

If only I had a bugle, he thought. But even if it would be fun to discomfit the rattled bandits with a few "Charge" and "Commence firing" calls, Slocum knew perfectly well that the cavalry would not be coming to the rescue this time. He cursed himself for not having planned ahead a little more. Why couldn't he have restrained his boyish high spirits and departed quietly?

As if that had been possible after Juan's last flight! But he could have spent a little more time preparing: dump a few boulders down into camp, build a few fires here and there, make a little more noise, and he could have spooked them, convinced them the whole motherless Union army was coming with the California Rangers just behind.

Mojave Joe's arms were around his waist and the old man was still howling in high glee. The situation did have its amusing aspects for everyone except Juan. Slocum thought it would be a lot funnier once he was well clear of this area and of Tiburcio Vásquez. Up ahead was a sudden flare. Now what innocent was rushing about with a torch, giving away his position and blinding himself?

The flare grew larger, and abruptly Slocum saw that Vásquez had been prepared. Someone had ignited a pile of brush. Other fires were starting up. He slowed Dorkus and glanced back. Fire behind them, too.

"What happens if we go that way?" He pointed into the deep woods.

"Me go good. Maybe you. But horse?"

Slocum was goddamned if would give up Dorkus again! He turned and forced the gelding through the brush. It made a lot of noise, but by now the camp was in an uproar and there were several shouting people up here on the rimrock. Somebody fired what sounded like a Sharps. Were they shooting at one another? There was the replying bellow of a *fusil* such as Slocum had not heard since the siege of Querétaro. He wondered if some pelón had deserted with full equipment. But mainly he wondered if it would be possible to force a horse and two riders through this forest. Had that been two trees, or had Dorkus split one? Why couldn't he have spread it a little wider and made room for Slocum's legs, too?

"Crazy sumbitch, you bet!"

Slocum was not inclined to argue.

Faint hints of moonlight filtered through the forest canopy, but they were blundering through nearly total darkness. Slocum could still hear the commotion, but, thank God, it was behind and growing fainter. "I hope there's a way out of here," he said.

"No way."

"What?"

"Okay me, maybe you. But a horse no climb down rope."

XI

They had ridden less than an hour, climbing higher into the mountains, Slocum thought, when Joe abruptly said "Go" and pointed toward a damp wash where *carrizos* grew as impenetrable as the canebrakes he had seen in some parts of the South. By the time they had forced the gelding halfway through, he was almost ready to agree with Mojave Joe about the usefulness of horses. At the moment, Dorkus was a nuisance; Slocum had to lead the horse, unless he was willing to lose even more skin than he had already lost escaping Vásquez. But finally they broke into a small clearing, and there was a trickle of clear water from the overhanging rock. "Vásquez got plenty place to hide," said Joe. "But Joe got couple more."

"He doesn't know about this place?"

"Vásquez like all Mexican. Horse no go, Vásquez no go."

Slocum suspected there was a moral somewhere in all this, but what it might be utterly escaped him. Mojave Joe was already wrapping his wrinkled body in a California blanket he had liberated from the Vásquez stronghold. Slocum wrapped up in his own newly recovered blankets, and they slept.

Slocum had a nightmare in which he was on the receiving end of a cannonade. He woke abruptly and was struck by the intensity of a dream that could make his ears ache. Then he saw Mojave Joe sitting up, too. "You bet. Le's go!"

It was still dark, but somewhere in the mountains lightning had struck. "What's the hurry?" Then he realized where they were. The bottom of a gully damp enough to grow *carrizos* was no place to be when uphill it was raining.

Men and horse were somewhat scratched by the time they blundered out through the *carrizos* and got back on the main trail through the mountains. He wondered if the Vásquez *bandidos* had got over their panic and found a new shelter. He hoped they would not be out prowling.

The first drops came pattering down through the pines and landed loudly on the trail, sending up little explosions of dust that made Dorkus skittish. Slocum studied the moon and guessed they had another half hour before it would be hidden by the western slope, if a thunderhead didn't blot it out sooner.

"Le's go," Joe urged.

Slocum didn't know what the hurry was. They were up out of the gully now, up where the trail crossed a hogback ridge. They would be wet, cold, buffeted by wind, but there promised nothing worse than the ordinary soldier's lot. Then, suddenly, he could feel every hair on his head and body standing on end.

Arms wrapped tightly around Slocum's waist, Mojave Joe sat pillion. "Le's—" Abruptly he broke off and began chanting. Slocum didn't know the language, but he had heard a death song before. Without thinking, he neck-reined Dorkus off the ridge and spurred, yelling and slapping his hat over the gelding's rump until it charged blindly down the forty-five-degree slope into the brush. Up on the ridge behind them the world came to an abrupt and fiery end.

The flash was blinding. The noise was like that of a powder magazine blowing up. Afterward, balls of fire rolled lazily about the place where the trail crossed the ridge. One came downhill toward them, and the gelding screamed. A ghostly ball of the lightning's mortal remains approached, stopped short, then peeled the bark from a bull pine. When the charge dissipated, Slocum's hair no longer stood on end.

"Crazy sumbitch!" Mojave Joe said. "You faster'n lightning."

Slocum seldom received compliments of this order. He sighed. If the lightning had served no other useful purpose, at least he was now thoroughly awake. So was the gelding. He spent several minutes talking the nonsense one uses to calm horses and women, and finally the beast promised to turn manageable as the storm blew over and gave them a glimpse of stars and a just-disappearing moon. "Got any idea where we are?" Slocum asked.

"You bet. Le's go."

He had come out here to find Laura. Now that he was no longer plagued with immediate threats to life and limb, the thought of the girl returned like a half-forgotten toothache. Had she gone, or had they taken her? Maybe he should have pried a little harder—made her tell him something more of her past. If he was to be completely in the dark about her problems, how was he to be of any help? Did she want any help? Did he want to drive himself mad thinking in circles like some diseased animal? He shook his head and stared up the trail. It was most ungodly dark now that the moon was down. He squinted through streaky clouds for a glimpse of the Dipper but couldn't find it in these mountains.

"Sun come soon," Joe said as he saw Slocum searching for a time star.

"How far's the Cross Seven?"

"You bet."

Slocum and Mojave Joe were by now so cold they could hardly sit the horse, and they slipped off to walk themselves warm again. They were still walking an hour later when the sun broke through the clouds. Slocum wondered if it might not be a good idea to halt now for coffee and pinole while the morning light was good enough to make a campfire invisible but not good enough to show smoke.

"No fire," Joe insisted.

"Vásquez?"

"Him, too."

"Are we that close to Cross Seven?"

"You bet."

"How close?"

Joe put a finger to his lips and pointed.

"My word!" Slocum muttered. A half mile ahead of them, silhouetted on the skyline, were the ears of a horse and the upper part of a man in a uniform Slocum was almost sure he recognized. The sentinel was scanning the area below him with field glasses. As Slocum watched, the glasses swept slowly toward where he and Mojave Joe stood in front of the tired gelding. He glanced at Joe. The Indian was gone.

Slocum was still trying to decide whether to make some signal or to make his way around this sentinel and avoid a lot of tiresome "Advance and be recognized" randygazoo when he heard an accented voice behind him. "Halt! Put up your hands!"

His mind had been made up for him. Slocum raised his hands. Moments later he was back aboard the gelding, blindfolded, being led over a trail that turned so many times that even with the warmth of the sun to one side Slocum could not really remember which way they were heading. He wondered if the Indian was already on his way back to Yuma and one of his wives.

They rode for the better part of an hour, and then he was ushered into a—what was it? His feet were still on hard-packed earth, but he could tell from the way voices echoed that they were under some kind of roof. Another ramada, he decided. The blindfold was pulled off, and a man with flowing mustache, in odd contrast to the tight ringlets of his short ginger hair and beard, was squinting at him from behind a makeshift table. "You're a white man," Ginger Hair accused. "What you doin' hangin' out with a greaser bandit like Vásquez?"

"Now, what on earth ever gave you that diverting idea?" Slocum asked. "Is this the Cross Seven? I'm looking for a gentleman of the French persuasion."

"Are you now? And what might his name be?"

"It might be General Lyautey, just as yours might be General Lee. But unless memory betrays me," Slocum elaborated, "you're Crow Crowley, on whose court-martial I once sat. Tell me, did you escape from a *juarista* prison, or did you buy your way out?"

Crowley ran a hand through kinky ginger hair and

squinted. "By God!" he muttered. "Are you the one who held out for conviction?"

"You'll never know, will you? But now that it's over, wasn't a trainload of Union gold enough? Did you really rob the passengers and impugn the honor of a Southern officer and gentleman?"

Crowley gave him a wolfish grin. " 'F it had been enough, we might've won, now, mightn't we?"

Slocum had given this problem considerable thought since the war ended and had belatedly concluded there was no way gallantry and discipline could have prevailed over unlimited cannon fodder and unlimited cannon. This was hardly the place to discuss it.

"Where'd you hear about Giraud?" Crowley asked.

"Same place I heard about you. Did you escape together?"

"Well, Slocum!" It was one of the poker players from San Bernardino, a graying, taciturn man who had offered no suggestions when Slocum sought information about the Cross Seven. Up here he seemed less reserved. " 'Pears like they couldn't keep a good man down."

Crowley glared, but the once-silent poker player continued imperturbably. "Slocum's the man who brought Miss van Arnem safe and sound 'crost Injun country."

Van Arnem. Slocum knew he had heard the name somewhere. But where? And why hadn't Laura trusted him enough to give her real name? He glanced around hoping for a glimpse of her, but there were only men in sight. A hundred yards behind the ramada was a pole corral and bunkhouse. Beyond that lay the great house, which was not all that great for a spread of this size. It was a compact cabin with sleeping loft, laid up out of pine logs only slightly thicker than lodgepoles, with the corners boarded and battened instead of notched, as was customary. Slocum considered the grass chinking and split shake roof. A proper firetrap, he concluded. How had it survived this long?

"I suppose you're here to join up," Crowley was saying, but Slocum's attention had wandered from the ginger-haired man. He stared at the doddering remnant of a man who emerged from the cabin. The wizened graybeard still wore the full uniform of a general in the Army of the Confederate States of America.

The old man walked hesitantly toward them, squinting into the sunlight. With each step his head jerked sideways in a ticlike movement, but as he approached, Slocum saw that the eyes were still bright and alert. Too bright. *"Attention!"* It was another of the poker players.

Crowley sprang from his chair and spun to face the old man. Without thinking, Slocum found himself saluting along with the rest of them. The old man returned the salute. "Stand at ease." His voice was cracked with age. He studied Slocum. "New, aren't you?"

"John Slocum, sir. Formerly Major, CSA."

"Formerly? You've been invalided out, then?"

Slocum shot a quick glance over the old man's head, but no one gave him a clue. "Not exactly, sir. My unit was disbanded some years ago."

"Sad. Chaos just when the South needs us most. But rest assured—Slocum, is it? This unit will never disband. Right shall prevail."

"I pray it may, sir." Slocum had a sudden suspicion. "Did Miss Laura sleep well?"

"My daughter's health is excellent, thank you." General van Arnem gave the staff a cursory review. "Carry on," he said. "And, Slocum, you come with me."

Crowley was frowning and shaking his head, but Slocum could hardly disobey a direct order from the general. He saluted and fell in beside the old man, one pace to the rear. They had almost reached the doorway of the cabin when Crowley trotted up and placed himself before the general. Saluting, he said, "I'm dreadful sorry, sir, but Slocum was in the midst of a report on the enemy's strength and position. I'm afraid we have immediate need for his information."

"Very well. See me when you've finished, young man."

"Yes, sir." Slocum wondered if this was Crowley's way of translating that Vásquez scrape into official terms.

"Should have seen the poor devil when my party rescued him," Crowley muttered as they walked back toward the ramada.

"Your party?" Slowly it was coming back to Slocum. Crowley had been one of Mosby's raiders. A rather successful one, in spite of his inability to distinguish between private property and legitimate spoils of war, which had brought protests and threats of retaliation against hostage Southerners. Slocum had always assumed he was guilty as charged, but in those final years of the war Confederate courts-martial had faced the dreadful choice between should and must. Crowley, Quantrill—how many others had put a permanent strain on Southern gallantry?

Finally, in those doom-filled days when it had all come apart, this ginger-haired man had been part of Jeff Davis's escort. That idealist had packed the remains of the Confederacy's treasury in wagons and headed south through occupied territory without friends, without destination, without hope. And of course they had all been captured, and of course they had all been imprisoned, and of course they had never been tried for any crime. How could a "union" seeking to reestablish itself continue for so long to treat a part of "itself" as the enemy?

A man in the remains of a Hapsburg legionnaire's uniform rode into camp. *"Bon jour, mon capitaine."* He saluted Crowley.

There was a lengthy report. Slocum did not speak French as well as he did Spanish, but he gathered that the usual Vásquez spies who hung about the fringes of Cross Seven were not at their customary posts and that there were indications that a large band had passed through the mountains in some confusion.

Crowley turned to Slocum. "You must've come from that way. What do you know about it?"

"You know where Vásquez's main camp is, then?"

"Do you?"

Slocum shrugged. "Few of them surprised me. Got my horse and kit."

"You had a horse when you came in here."

"Also a fair amount of my kit."

Crowley gave him a searching look, but Slocum volunteered nothing more. "Hope you'll be as close-mouthed about our affairs," the ginger-haired man finally muttered.

"Surely your whereabouts are known?"

"But not our purpose."

Slocum waited, but this time it was Crowley who volunteered nothing more. "You did rescue the general?"

"Oh, yes. The Yankees kept the old man locked up on Dry Tortugas along with Dr. Mudd and a few others for years after the war was over. No matter what they tried, the old man never talked. It would have been better for him if he had."

"Perhaps he recognized the nature of a life sentence to live with oneself."

Crowley gave a wolfish grin. "They were taking him to Biloxi. They intended a face-to-face with Jeff Davis to see if a direct order from his old commander-in-chief would make him spill the beans."

"Apparently it did not."

Crowley grinned. "Somewhere between Fort Jefferson and Biloxi the navy lost custody of their prisoner."

"I see," Slocum said. But he didn't see at all. What purpose could be served by holding an inoffensive man well beyond retirement age in a hellhole that made Andersonville look like a summer retreat?

"Nor will he talk to us," Crowley said. "So, I regret that I must insist that you tell us. Major Slocum, just where is the gold?"

XII

Slocum stared. "What gold?"

"You crossed the country with Miss van Arnem."

"Quite right," Slocum admitted. "But you and I are not the only closemouthed people on this desolated patch of mud."

"She didn't tell you?"

"Until a moment ago I didn't even know her true name."

Crowley surveyed him doubtfully. "Are you subject to the same aches and desires as normal men?"

"I don't slaver over fat little boys, if that's what you're getting at!"

The ginger-haired man shook his head. "So you know nothing about gold?"

"I wouldn't mind having a ton or two."

"Then you're among your own kind." Crowley sighed and looked for a shaded place beneath a huge sugar pine. "There might be *several* tons," he said.

Slocum looked at him incredulously. "Sure. Long tons, or short tons? Or metric?"

"As you wish," Crowley said. "It actually began much earlier, but I may as well start with the civil war in Spain."

Oh, my God, Spanish gold! If I don't keep both hands on my poke, he'll have me anteing up next to buy out a Spanish prisoner. But Slocum limited his observations to asking, "Which civil war?"

Crowley shrugged. "Actually, I expect it began in the seventeen hundreds with the suppression of the Jesuits. You could call that a civil war of a sort. In any event, the Jesuits were ordered to leave California and give their missions over to another order. Oddly enough, they decided not to hand over all their treasure. They buried much of it. Some has remained buried for over a hundred years."

One hundred three, unless Slocum was subtracting wrong.

"But the Jesuits have to survive just as the rest of us," Crowley continued. "They backed the Carlist side during the last civil war."

"Figures," Slocum agreed. "One lot's about as die-hard as t'other."

"And they told the *carlistas* about the hidden gold in California."

Slocum's antennae began quivering. But he, too, had heard many stories about hidden gold. "What part of California?"

"You're getting extremely warm," Crowley said. "You knew about our alliance with Spain, I gather."

"Helps explain why we lost the war."

"Well, Palmerston certainly wasn't doing much for us in England. We were forced to take any help we could get. I expect the *carlistas* felt the same way. In any event, they sent a representative to conclude a deal with President Davis."

"That I didn't know. . . . Are you sure of all this?"

"Chapter and verse," Crowley snapped. "Don't forget that I was there."

Slocum spread his hands. "So, to my infinite regret, was I."

"On Jefferson Davis's staff?"

"Your hand."

"And I plan to keep it that way."

"Was General van Arnem on Davis's staff, too?"

Crowley ignored the question. "They had us blockaded by then—everything but the *Alabama* and a few runners. The Carlist agent couldn't get out of Cuba, so Davis sent van Arnem to meet him there. I was the military escort."

"The light begins to dawn," Slocum said. "So naturally you know precisely where the gold is buried."

"I wasn't present at the meeting. There were Union

spies all over Havana, and I was busy protecting the general from them." Crowley shrugged. "It was my duty."

Slocum started to laugh, then realized it wasn't funny. Crowley didn't look like a man who took honor seriously, but then neither did Slocum. It wasn't far-fetched at all to imagine Captain Crowley ready to die for the Southern cause. Slocum had been, and had almost managed it several times. He fingered the scar beneath his hair.

"So we returned," Crowley said. "The general saw no reason to tell me; nor could I really blame him. And of course we came back to chaos. Sherman was moving east from Atlanta. Grant was moving steadily. By the time we returned to Richmond, all the gold in the world wouldn't have saved the South."

Slocum was puzzled. He had all the facts, and still the story didn't make sense. "Why haven't you dug it up and used it?"

"Jeff Davis only knew there was Jesuit gold. He never knew where."

"But van Arnem—"

"—was a brave and honest soldier who never did anything to merit being locked up on Dry Tortugas with Dr. Mudd or any of the other decent people who died for a noble cause."

"Dr. Mudd was guilty of nothing."

"Neither was the general. But you've seen him. Seven years those Yankee bastards cooped him up in a dungeon and fed him slop. Seven years they tormented him, but the old man held his tongue. He'll tell us in his own good time, he says. And only when he's certain it will be used properly." Crowley paused. "Properly means to help the South rise again, of course."

Slocum groaned. The South was rising, in a totally unexpected way now that the carpetbaggers and all the Northern rascals had been booted out. But it would never be like the old days of glory. "Doesn't he know how things are?"

"Without a newspaper, a light, or a pair of spectacles?" Crowley controlled himself. "At any event, the Pinkertons learned of the gold, possibly in Havana. There were certainly enough of them there. Allan Pinkerton told Congressman Stevens. Need I say more?"

"I think not," Slocum said. Stevens was the most spiteful and backbiting of all the Northern legislators who wished to see the South permanently destroyed. There were those—and they were a majority in Washington—who thought his ideas stemmed mainly from his black "housekeeper." But at least the old reprobate had been constant enough over the last thirty years not to turn her in for a new one each season.

"They were shipping the old man from Fort Jefferson on Dry Tortugas to Biloxi. As I understand it, if President Davis would give the general a direct order to tell where the gold was, then maybe they'd get around to releasing Davis."

"Or at least charging him with something," Slocum murmured. "But I still don't see where you come in."

"President Davis had been permitted an orderly," Crowley said. "A sergeant who had formerly served General van Arnem and who was at one time in my troop with Mosby. He wanted to see his general freed."

"And you intercepted a U.S. Navy warship."

"A very small one. And of course I had the help of a remnant of our late Emperor Maximilian's forces, including one of his naval vessels that turned pirate rather than surrender to the *juaristas*." Crowley grinned wickedly. "I must say I enjoyed the experience of outgunning a Yankee. It happened so seldom during the war."

"This just barely makes sense. After all you did, the general still won't tell you where the gold is?"

"He says it is not yet time." Crowley made a corkscrew motion at his temple. "We thought perhaps he was waiting to be certain his daughter was safe. He spoke of her constantly. I had hoped the girl would have told you by now."

"Does she know?"

Crowley was suddenly uncertain; then he brightened. "Even if she doesn't, she can work on the old man and get him to tell us."

"What're you going to do with it?"

Crowley shrugged. "We must be realists. The cause is doomed, and all the gold in the world won't restore the Confederacy." He paused, and when Slocum said nothing, he added, "What will you do with your share?"

Slocum had not even known of the gold's existence a moment ago. "Assuming I get a cut, I guess I might try South America. Or perhaps Australia. New Zealand sounds a bit too full of sheep, but it'd be nice to speak English, real English, not that Gatling-gun Yankee variety."

Crowley grinned as he got to his feet. "You know what you must do to earn your cut, I suppose."

"Reckon so."

"Just get the information. Oh, and I don't like to be indelicate, but the sentries would very much resent it if you tried to leave camp without my permission. Surely you won't find that an inconvenience."

"I'll get used to it."

"Splendid." Crowley grinned again and strode back to his table and chair beneath the ramada.

Slocum got to his feet and strolled thoughtfully around behind the boars' nest where men were lining up for tin plates of something that smelled like food. When Slocum had worked his way up the line, he surveyed the dipperful of brownish muck that smelled of pumpkin and grits and gave it the benefit of the doubt. He found a shady place and sat down to eat.

"That's my spot." The voice sounded Missouri or Arkansas.

Slocum looked up from his half-finished plate. "Be on my way in a moment," he said.

" 'Fraid that ain't fast enough." The man wore faded gray with the three stripes of a sergeant.

"Very well." Slocum stood and used the tin plate to trowel the remainder of his dinner as evenly as he could across a scowling face. "Is that fast enough?"

The Missouri or Arkansas sergeant took a second to realize this was really happening. He squinted through pumpkin and grits at the hand that hovered near a pistol. He decided it was entirely too fast. Amid hoots and bravos he retreated. And now Slocum knew he would have another reason to watch his back. Why couldn't he be peaceable and settle these things like other men? But men who tried to settle these things peaceably didn't seem to do that much better than Slocum.

"Tu iras loin," a graying man in Legion uniform observed.

"I've already gone far," Slocum said. "Been hoping I could slow down and settle down."

"Aussi un légionnaire du bas?"

"Yes, I was down there, too. After the emperor died at Querétaro they locked a bunch of us up in the dungeon at Perote."

"Pardon?"

"Perote. 'Bout halfway down the mountains on the road from Puebla to Veracruz. Charming place if you don't mind a litle mold and moss on the walls." He saw the Frenchman's puzzled air and did not elaborate on how he had spent the first month deciphering the inscriptions of some Texans who had stayed there a generation earlier.

"¿Habla español?"

"Somewhat better than French," Slocum replied. *"¿Y usted?"*

The graying man shrugged, and after that their conversation was not so blatantly at cross-purposes. "How did your contingent get free of the *juaristas?"* Slocum asked. "Bribes, or escape?"

The graying man rubbed his scalp. *"Je ne sais pas,"* he admitted. "One night there were no sentries, and we escaped. From the ease with which we made our way out of the city . . ." He shrugged.

"To what end was this garrison formed?" Slocum asked.

"A man must live."

"Cattle?"

"A few. Mostly, we keep the road open between San Bernardino and the coast; the ranchers pay us to keep the road safe from Vásquez. But they do not pay enough, so we cut firewood and *traverses* for the *chemin de fer.*"

"Traverses?"

There being no railroad in Mexico, the Frenchman did not know the Spanish word. He explained and pantomimed.

"Durmientes," Slocum said. "Same as the English 'sleepers.' But in this country they're 'cross ties.' "

"Ah."

"But armies do not live by cutting wood."

"You have a war for us to fight?"

Slocum did not. The legionnaire shrugged and lit a vile clay pipe. Slocum moved toward fresher air.

Beautiful day up here in the mountains, mockingbirds and jays whooping it up, woodpeckers breaking off long enough to chase away a crow. High above, two bee martens were taking turns harassing an eagle. Every one of God's creatures had something to pick on, but not Crowley's ragtag army. It puzzled Slocum.

"Major Slocum!"

He turned at the sound of a woman's voice. "Oh, my, aren't we formal today!" It was Laura.

She shook her head slightly and struggled to warn him. Barely in time Slocum, managed to control himself. A moment later General van Arnem stepped from behind a tree. Slocum saluted. "Sir."

"Stand at ease. Major, my daughter speaks well of you. She has told me that you rescued her from savages after Sergeant Major MacFarlane was killed and that you brought her here even though you did not know her name or why she wanted to come to this place."

"Yes, sir—"

"Also that you wish to speak to me regarding her future."

"Yes, sir; that, too. I—I regret the deplorable state my clothing—"

The general smiled faintly. "You do not much resemble a major of cavalry at present, but of course we must not reveal ourselves just yet. Laura, you are excused."

She looked helplessly at Slocum, then back to her father. "Yes, sir," she said finally, and left.

"Tell me, young man, have you been home recently?" van Arnem asked.

Slocum looked carefully at the old man. He still wore the uniform, faded gold lace and all, but the mad gleam Slocum had seen earlier in his eyes seemed to have vanished. "Sir, my home ceased to exist some years ago. The property has changed hands so many times that it's unclear whether the present owners are scoundrels or victims."

The general nodded absently. "My daughter has told me of conditions at home. Our people crushed beneath the conqueror's heel! But we will rise and throw off the oppressor! Mark my words, young man. There will be a new Confederacy. A new day will dawn!"

"Takes money," Slocum said. "And before tackling the Yankees again, I'd like to have at least one cannon foundry within our national borders. It would have helped if we'd had a proper navy, so we could draw on all the European countries for cannon fodder."

"I expect I know more of that than you," van Arnem said. "I was largely concerned with trying to supply them. Unsuccessfully, of course. Tell me, Major, if I give my consent to this marriage, how do you propose to support Laura?"

Slocum frowned. Was van Arnem sane or not? What did he want to hear? "I guess I have to say, just the best way I can," Slocum finally said.

"And our cause?"

"Sir, the war is over. We lost it. How could we start again? Parts of the South are still occupied. Carpetbaggers and the Freedman's Bureau control [illegible] the local governments. The slaves are free—"

"I freed my slaves the day the war began," van Arnem said. "Most stayed with me to the end. Unlike General Forrest, I was not fighting to keep my niggers. Major Slocum, I know it will not be easy—but we do have a start. Money. We will soon have a very great deal of money."

"Then there really is some hidden gold?"

"The United States Congress was sufficiently convinced to bury and torment me for seven years. Were it not for Captain Crowley, I might still be their captive."

When he put it that way, Slocum had to agree it sounded convincing. "And when do we recover this gold?"

"Very soon. I have waited to hear from Laura, and now that is accomplished. Major, when we have the money, will you support the cause?"

Slocum had to think how to answer that. "General, I just don't know. It depends on what that support would be. I do not think there is much chance of an armed revolt no matter how much Carlist gold there is—"

"Perhaps not," van Arnem said. "But with sufficient money there is always something to be accomplished. Politicians can be bought. Have you not considered that we can establish a base, not in this country?"

Slocum had heard of other filibuster expeditions, to Central America and elsewhere. Cuba was ripe for plucking from Spain. And what then?

Van Arnem looked very old and tired. "I may not live to see the end of it—but you will." Suddenly the old general was pleading. "Major Slocum, I only know that we have an opportunity which should not be abandoned lightly. As my daughter's husband you will be my heir. I hope I can trust you."

"You can trust me to do what I think is right, General. But I have to say that I don't at the moment know what that would be."

"That, I think, is all I can ask for," van Arnem said. He smiled faintly. "At least I know that you did not court my daughter for her money. Now, let us go find Captain Crowley. I see no point in further delay."

"By ginger, for a man who didn't know diddly, you sure wormed it out of him quick enough!" Crowley said enthusiastically.

Slocum smiled and struggled to conceal his puzzlement. He hadn't wormed anything at all out of poor old General van Arnem.

Had he simply been waiting for his daughter, or had she actually borne some secret message? And if she had, was there really— For an instant Slocum's heart leaped with the hope that the South might truly rise again. Then he remembered where he was: a ranch in the mountains of California with a ragtag assortment of hardcase losers from every war of the last twenty years. Losers, every one of them. Many of them, like himself, had managed to pick the losing side twice in a row. Served him right for trying to restore order in a country with a congenital dislike for any sensible, orderly way of doing things.

"We'll ride immediately. Get in a good ten miles before sundown."

"Your deal," Slocum said. "But before we ride, how're you fixed for sidearms?"

Crowley smoothed his flowing ginger mustache. "Who needs 'em?"

"I do. Got my mount and part of my kit back, but Vásquez ran for it before I could recover my pistols."

"Giraud!"

Moments later the leader of the French contingent of Emperor Maximilian's army appeared. *"Mon capitain?"*

"Cap'n Giraud, this is Major Slocum. The general has seen fit to tell him the location of the gold. See if you can find him a decent set of pistols."

"Avec plaisir, mon capitaine."

It was an hour before they were ready to break

camp, late enough so that anywhere else it wouldn't have been worth the bother; but here it was a relatively short ride down out of an alpine paradise into the nearest branch office of hell. The men could take the abrupt change, but it was hell on the horses. If they rode down out of the mountains tonight, then rested through the hottest part of tomorrow, the beasts would have a better chance of living in the desert.

"Your weapons, Mr. Slocum."

"Uh, yes, thank you, Captain. Giraud, isn't it?"

"Of Marseille, Algérie, Mexique, *et* Californie."

"Et de l'or?"

"Non. Mon— Slocum, I am *from* all those places, but I go *to* the gold. How do you like the pistols?"

"Almost like my own."

Giraud shrugged. "Someday perhaps we shall kill Vásquez. But then, with enough gold it is difficult to become excited over the problems of Vásquez and the locals."

"A profound observation," Slocum agreed as he belted on the pair of Colts. Once they hung properly, he drew one and fired into the air. The cap popped. He sighed and snapped off all six caps. Five fired, but only one chamber ignited, and its powder was so damp that it only squibbed. He cursed and began picking at the dried and cracking tallow that was supposed to prevent this. It was hard to tell how long it had been since these weapons had been fired.

Save for Laura, the general, and a half dozen sentinels, the Cross Seven riders had mounted en masse and were half an hour down the trail, with Slocum straggling until he finished picking the patches and balls from both weapons, augering a piece of wire through caked powder until he could clear a way toward the nipple, then recharge each chamber with enough fresh powder to burn out this caked saltpeter. Finally, both pistols were cleaned, the nipples reamed and reloaded to his satisfaction. He spurred toward the head of the column and only then noted the pair of riders who had been detailed to lag behind and make sure he didn't "stray."

"Must've been somewhere along here you came up against Vásquez," Crowley said, greeting him.

"Looks pretty much the same after dark. Going to ride all night?"

"Sore butt tonight or sunstroke *mañana.*" The ginger-haired man broke off at the sound of shooting up at the point.

XIII

"Now what the hell?" Crowley growled.

Moments later the point man had dropped back. "Be goldanged if I know," he said. " 'F I didn't know they ain't no hostiles around here, I'd swear it was an Injun."

"Did you get him?"

The point man shook his head. "Scampered off right spry for such a wrinkled old bastard."

"Why'd you shoot?" Slocum asked.

The point man held up an arrow. "Came so close it seemed downright unfriendly."

Slocum wondered what Mojave Joe was up to now. Playing tag with a lone dismounted man was one thing. This was downright foolishness. What did the Indian want?

"Ever see an arrow like that before?" Crowley asked.

Slocum studied the point, which was crude and totally unlike those flinty *objets d'art* that came to be known as Folsom points. "Believe I saw one once," he admitted. "Little ways from here, though." While Crowley shrugged, Slocum amused himself by thinking that he had told nothing but the unadorned truth. Maybe he should take up lawyering. They made a profession of turning little truths into big lies.

The night wore on, and the seat of Slocum's breeches wore thinner. It was nearing dawn before he realized that they were not going into the kind of country he had expected. Instead of dropping into the desert floor, they wound through mountains, climbing steadily until at points the pines grew bushy and gnarled. They camped that forenoon in a broad meadow on the shore of a mountain lake.

Slocum decided that he'd been had. There was no

reason for not traveling daytimes in country as cool and pleasant as this—unless General van Arnem's brigade had good reason to stay hidden. He studied the sixty-odd men. Vásquez's force was smaller. The nearest detachment of the U.S. Army was a hundred miles and more away. Just whom were they avoiding?

"You carry no rifle." Giraud had worked his way up the file to ride beside Slocum. The sun was still a few minutes above the mountains.

Slocum was startled. He had been so caught up in events that he had forgotten the heavy, telescope-sighted buffalo gun. Where had it gone to? Then he remembered. The buffalo gun and Mojave Joe had disappeared at about the same time. Slocum wondered if Joe knew how to use it—and what he wanted to use it on.

"I, uh, never was much of a shot with the things," Slocum said. "Do you know this country well?"

Giraud shrugged. "As well as one may in the two years I have passed here."

"How far is it to the river?" As there was only one river in these parts, Slocum meant the Colorado, which at this point divided the state of California from the Territory of Arizona.

"Directement, four days on a good horse and carrying water. In winter, of course. This time of year no one tries to cross the desert without mule teams and water wagons."

"But in winter how does one cross the river?"

"There are ferries at Yuma and Ehrenburg. Even in summer the water is of hazard."

"Then there's no way to cross this far north?"

Giraud shrugged again. *"C'est dangereux.* A good man on a good horse might swim the river. Sometimes there are passing boats. I think there is a ferry farther to the north. But generally there is no way."

Slocum filed the knowledge and wondered if it would ever prove useful. He remembered the rather prissy Irishman who had struggled to force mathematics into his horse-obsessed brain. "There is no such thing as useless information," that long-suffering worthy had insisted. Professor Moriarty had finally confessed the impossibility of his task to Slocum's father and shortly afterward departed. They had received one letter in which he spoke glowingly of his prospects with some English great house. Slocum struggled irrelevantly to remember the name. Homes or some such.

The sun rose higher, and they rode on.

They stopped for frequent conferences over the sketch map van Arnem had given them. There were no bearings, and it was difficult to know if the trail they followed led to an abandoned mission or merely wound through the mountains. Finally they crossed a ridge.

A crow gave raucous protest at the column's intrusion. Slocum glanced up quickly. It really was a crow, and not Mojave Joe having more fun. Up ahead, Crowley shouted orders. The column halted.

Slocum rode up to join Crowley. They had halted in a low depression. Silently, Crowley indicated the trail ahead.

At one time there had been a mine here. The head frame had long rotted away, leaving only outlines in thicker grass. The shaft had caved in.

Slocum studied a scrub oak that grew from the depression where the shaft had been. It collected water, and the stirred-up earth had made growth easier. He had seen how close together were the rings in California oak; that tree had been at least a century old when the Jesuits were forced out of California. He pointed at the depression.

"No use digging there," he told Crowley.

The Southerner nodded.

"So where?" Slocum asked.

Crowley passed Slocum the general's map. Those instructions had gone from California to Rome, from Rome to Spain, had passed from Jesuit to Carlist to Confederate and finally worked their way back to their place of origin. "One hundred paces from the larger oak toward the *aliso,* then right twelve paces," Slocum read. It seemed straightforward enough, except that there were neither large oaks nor alders. The only tree within the scope of the scribbled map was the scrub oak within the collapsed shaft. "I had a feeling that it would end this way," John said.

Crowley snorted in contempt. "Do you truly believe that the Jesuits would try to swindle President Davis when he would know the truth long before they could get any help from him? Their plan was for the South to win the war with the help of their gold, so that they would have Confederate aid in putting the *carlistas* back on the Spanish throne."

"It does seem odd when you put it that way," John said.

"So, think: if you were a Jesuit, where would you hide your gold?"

It was difficult enough for Slocum to imagine himself a Jesuit—yet the Jesuits were certainly as soldierly as they were devout, and Slocum had had enough experience in soldiering. He dismounted and wandered around the remains of the mining community. The others dismounted also. Soon the small depression was filled with men seeing to their horses, removing their boots, disappearing into the brush with handfuls of dry grass.

There was a row of low rectangles that had once been adobe houses. Downhill slightly from the caved-in shaft was the *arrastra,* a round pit lined with smooth rocks. Slocum had seen those devices working in Mexico; otherwise he'd never have been able to guess the use of that stone-lined pit. As he studied it, he knew where he would have buried gold if ever he'd possessed enough to worry about. He wondered if a Jesuit mind were more devious than his own.

"Where's the last place you'd think of looking for it?" he asked Crowley.

"If I knew, would I trouble you with the question?"

"Where do you think Poe would have put it?"

Being a Southerner, Crowley had read the works of that other Southerner who had created the mystery story. " 'The Purloined Letter'? In plain sight?"

Slocum pointed.

"And what is that?" Crowley asked.

"*Arrastra.* You never saw one working in Mexico?"

Crowley shook his head. "My part in that disaster was mostly confined to Mexico City."

"The hole in the middle is the bottom pivot. It once had a vertical wooden axle and a beam lashed crossways so that a mule—they blind them sometimes—can walk around and around the pit. Hook a ton-sized boulder to the cross beam and you have a fairly efficient ore crusher."

Crowley laughed. "It will never replace stamp mills."

"There weren't any stamp mills in California when this mine was operating."

"No, I suppose not. And you think the priests buried the gold there?"

"Know a better place?"

"No. We shall certainly try it." Crowley shouted orders.

While the troopers took turns barring out the smooth rocks, Slocum saw to his pistols. He moved to the edge of the clearing and chose a lightning-blazed pine to check the accuracy of the new Colts. His first shot went where he wanted it. A hundred crows exploded into flight, and from across the valley another flock rose to greet them. Slocum tried the second pistol, then, satisfied, reloaded and returned to where Crowley and Giraud were supervising the excavation.

The ground beneath the smoothed stones was soft and easily dug. The trooper in the hole was nearly invisible, his presence proved mostly by the shovelfuls of dirt which erupted onto a growing pile.

"I hit something!" The trooper's voice was shrill with excitement.

The officers bent over the hole, dodging back as another shovelful of dirt flew upward. "Roots," Slocum muttered.

Crowley peered into the hole.

Slocum shrugged. "Roots, or rock, or—"

Moments later the whole group knew it was gold.

For a moment Slocum would have bet that the people of San Bernardino also knew. Gradually the shouting died down and they got back to the serious business of counting small, roughly ounce-sized ingots of California gold. Each ingot was marked with a cross and crown and the letters "SJ": his Catholic Majesty of Spain and the Society of Jesus. Slocum wondered which of the two claimants had precedence, then laughed. Neither: the gold was now in the hands of Protestants. Or worse.

Somewhere beyond the edge of the mining campsite a crow cawed. Then suddenly crows were chorusing all around them. "For what we are about to receive, may we be truly thankful," Slocum muttered.

Crowley gave Slocum a startled look, then listened to the crows again. "God save us," he muttered. Then he shouted, "Dig in! Take cover!"

It was too late. Rifles were firing into them from all sides.

Slocum dived into the depression where the oak grew from the abandoned mineshaft. Immediately he wished he had not, as troopers began piling in on top of him. It was hard to catch his breath at the bottom of the human pile.

At least it's safe from bullets, he thought. Now what? Blood filtered down from above him, along with other fluids he preferred not to think about; the men were realizing just how exposed their position was. "Some days you just can't make a dime," Slocum muttered.

Topside, Crowley and Giraud were shouting orders. "Anybody want my place down here?" Slocum shouted. "Anybody wants it, move so I can get out." To his surprise it worked, and he scrambled out of the depression and ran toward Crowley.

The troopers had got over their surprise and now looked like legionnaires; they were firing methodically, concentrating on reloading properly and taking proper aim. Slocum ran past them and leaped onto his horse. A dozen troopers followed, and Slocum emitted a rebel yell.

New troops hid, but Slocum had learned early on to heed a bemedaled old drill sergeant's advice. "You hear dat twumpet, poy, you *chump!* First man scare dem so dey can't hit him. Den dey get set and shoot half the men behindt. But they neffer shot diss hero."

Crowley and Giraud were still whipping their men into shape when Slocum tore past yodeling his rebel yell with half a dozen men galloping behind him. Immediately Crowley's and Giraud's men joined the charge. Crowley and Giraud galloped alongside, struggling to flank their own men and reach the head of the column. They were beginning to draw conclusions about Slocum's forebears.

But though he might seem Southern gallantry personified, Slocum lay very close to the neck of his gelding, not attempting to draw a pistol. He concentrated on making speed straight ahead toward the enemy. Just who the hell was attacking them? Then he caught sight of ragged uniforms. Damned if they didn't look like *pelones!*

Part of the swarthy company that fired from well-prepared positions wore the cone shako of Mexican infantrymen. Others wore the *sombreros anchos* common in the south. The exaggeratedly wide hats were rare in California.

The charge had caught them between volleys. The *pelones* hastily reloaded and fired even more hastily. Mexican irregulars had never been noted for their accuracy, and hasty fire didn't improve it. Slocum heard bullets whistle past, but nothing touched him or his horse. Behind him men were picking up on the rebel yell. He remembered how effective it had been on occasion down there when it had been necessary to dislodge *juaristas* from a superior position. Abruptly one chord of the rebel yell behind him was cut off in mid-breath. At least one of the *pelones* knew how to aim his piece.

He was close to the lines now. Slocum drew one Colt and fired point-blank into a face that frowned as it struggled to skewer him on a tricornered bayonet. His gelding broke stride as its hoof skidded through flesh.

And as suddenly as it began, his charge ended. He was through the lines and picking away at them from behind while the *pelones* scurried and were unable to devote full attention to the river of men who followed Slocum. A *teniente* in white trousers strode up and down the firing line, bullying and whacking stray troops back into position with the flat of his sword. Slocum aimed a Colt, and the lieutenant sat heavily. If Slocum had been counting correctly, there were three shots left in his left-hand pistol. He swung Dorkus away from the action and began reloading.

God damn it, why couldn't they come up with a cartridge for pistols as they had for rifles? He spilled powder from shaking hands, dropped patches, had to dismount and pick up his pokeful of ball. Finally, all six chambers were charged, patched, ball rammed home, tallow stuffed into the end of the cylinder lest the first shot flash across and fire all six shots at once. He pressed a cap into each nipple and holstered the gun, then went to work on the other.

But a wounded *pelón* who had fallen back from the firing line had only one patch to cut for his weapon. Slocum glanced around just in time to see the *mestizo* aiming from behind a rock, butting the *fusil* to his unbloodied left shoulder. John dropped his ball poke again in his haste to draw the loaded Colt. And then he had to reload two chambers in that one along with three in his left-hand pistol. Slocum dismounted, picked up his poke of ball, and started over. There had to be a better way than this.

The goddamn *pelón* wouldn't die. He had been wounded before Slocum put two Colt balls into him. Still he struggled to reach the *fusil*. Abruptly Slocum realized he had not seen that weapon go off. He swung down from the gelding and captured the weapon. He drove the bayonet through the still-game *pelón,* then turned to see where best he might devote its single ball.

What in hell kind of a force was this? At least a third of them wore shiny black infantry shakos, but they could not have got so deep into this country without horses. And what the hell were Mexican soldiers doing two hundred miles inside the United

States? And if they weren't Mexican troopers, just who were they?

Vásquez? Not possible, Slocum decided. For one thing, there were entirely too many *pelones*. Some totally new faction had bought into the game. But just as abruptly they were buying out.

On the far side of the mining camp another column of Crowley's men were charging toward a blue GUADALUPANA banner. There was a cracked bugle call and the banner disappeared. Instantly a similar banner appeared on another hillside. "Rally round the flag, boys," Slocum muttered. Whoever these Mexicans were, their officers had realized that they'd lost the advantage of surprise, and now the battle had all the makings of a disaster.

Slocum emptied one pistol into fleeing *pelones;* then the rout topped the next rise to a line of picketed horses, and the infantry suddenly became cavalry. Slocum turned his tired horse. By the time he reached the safety of the Crowley-Giraud forces, the Mexicans had used their fresh horses to make good their withdrawal, leaving a thin screen behind to cover them.

"Let them go," Crowley said.

"Sure. But who the hell were they?" Slocum demanded. "And how did they know to follow us?"

"I should think you would recognize the uniforms," Crowley said. "And it seems obvious that we are not the only ones who know about Jesuit gold."

"So you don't know any more about it than I do?" Slocum asked.

"No."

"Still seems strange," Slocum said. "By the way, I presume you still have the gold?"

XIV

"Fear not," Crowley said with a laugh. "I'd spare a couple of inches sooner'n give that up."

"Greater love hath no man," Slocum observed.

"We paid for it."

"What was the butcher's bill?" Slocum asked.

"Five dead, and two more who will be. Six wounded who will probably recover."

"High enough," Slocum said. "How much did we get for our trouble?"

Crowley frowned. "Not as much as I'd expected."

"And how much might that be?"

"Rumor had it at a cool ten million. Unless I'm way off, my guess is there isn't more than half a million here."

"Isn't that cool enough?"

"Divided up, it comes to several thousand each for the men, and perhaps twenty thousand each for the officers. Not the earth, but something."

"Assuming it's to be divided."

Crowley gave him an odd look. "I suppose you're still saving your Confederate money?"

"I scarcely know what to do with all my Hapsburg pay warrants. But what will the general have to say about it?"

"Yes," Crowley said thoughtfully. "There is that to consider. But I point out that half a million dollars, while quite a lot to us, is very short of what would be needed to start a new War for Southern Independence. Perhaps the general will see reason."

"And if he doesn't?"

"I expect we'll have to cross that bridge when we come to it, won't we."

They organized the column into march order, with advance and rear guards, flankers, and scouts. Crowley and Giraud stayed near the gold—and near each other. Slocum could already feel the tension among the men. What was it about gold that did that to people?

Idly, Slocum speculated on his chances of ever seeing an ounce of it. Two days ago he had not even known there was any gold. He wondered how many other men in camp were speculating on how much a soldier's share would turn out to be. For some, anything would be welcome. For others, all of it would not be enough. And for Slocum? Twenty thousand dollars would buy a ranch. Add the general's share, assuming that van Arnem would choose to live with his daughter and son-in-law, and Slocum would be a long way toward landed respectability.

If he could trust Giraud and Crowley to deal fairly.

There was plenty of time to think about the situation as they made their way back to the ranch. Despite the watchfulness of the scouts, they saw no sign of the Mexican force. At nightfall they made camp near the lake, with guards posted in trios. Slocum found a level spot and laid out his blanket roll.

Sleep wouldn't come. There was too much tension in the camp. Gold, Slocum thought. Gold and the Mexicans.

He wondered if the Mexicans had always known about the gold but, like Crowley, had been stuck for an exact location. In a way it was too bad the Mexicans hadn't found it before Crowley. It had been the Spaniards who first sweated the Indians for the gold; now Spanish settler and Indian had melded into *mestizo,* and their claim was several degrees closer than Crowley's or the Confederacy's. But the trouble with situations like this was that just as in war, somebody had to lose. In spite of having led the charge that saved the situation, Slocum suspected he was going to lose.

They would give him a handshake, a pat on the back, a pair of pistols or a gold watch. But perhaps not. It all depended on how much honor Crowley and

Giraud had left. They'd started as honorable men. . . .

So had I, Slocum thought. And now? He remembered another Laura, Lieutenant Kenton's wife at the place everyone called Fort Hades. I didn't act very honorably there, he thought. And neither did Kenton.

He wrapped his blanket against the chill at this altitude and waited for morning. Toward dawn he had dropped off into troubled sleep when he was awakened by distant gunfire.

He sighed and burrowed deeper, waiting to see if it would turn into a full-scale battle. The firing died away, and Slocum decided he could wait until sunup to find out what had happened, but before he could sleep again, he heard Crowley's voice. "Slocum?"

"Over here."

"Another of those damned arrows. I don't suppose you have any idea who's doing it?"

"I've been here less than a week," Slocum protested as he looked at Mojave Joe's arrow. "Why should I know more about the local savages than you?"

"There aren't any local savages," Crowley said. "The nearest hostiles would be Apaches, and they're on the other side of the river. Unless someone has led a war party here—"

"Was anyone hurt?" Slocum asked.

"No. That's the strange part of it. The pickets say the arrow came between them. As if someone were trying to scare them."

"Our Mexican friends?" Slocum said, yawning.

"I noticed no Indians among the *juaristas.*"

"Oh, is *that* who they were?"

"I expect so. Juárez's followers have lost most of their influence now that President Benito is dead. Possibly they believe that with enough gold they can go home and spike Díaz's guns."

"Who?"

"General Porfirio Díaz. Don't you follow the politics down there? While Juárez was alive, Díaz made nothing but trouble for him. Then the old buck died suddenly and Don Porfirio found himself in the embarrassing position of having intrigued against the man with his picture on all the postage stamps. Díaz must have shed ten gallons of tears while laying wreaths on the old Indian's tomb."

"So who's running the *juaristas* now?"

Crowley shrugged. "Díaz has been pretty sharp about weeding out the opposition. About the only one in his way now is Bernardo Reyes, who's a little too big to touch. Perhaps him, perhaps some village *jefe* who fancies himself the new savior. *¿Quien sabe?*"

"But you are certain those weren't Díaz's people who attacked us?"

"Yes. They rake in half a million in bribes every week. I cannot think Don Porfirio would risk awakening the American *federales* by sending regular army units across our borders. Compared to what that bandit already takes, our little hoard is small potatoes indeed."

"Please," Slocum protested. "Once a bandit succeeds in stealing a whole country, he becomes a liberator. And as of this moment, you've almost enough gold to become a Yankee."

"You're forgetting General van Arnem."

Slocum looked at Crowley.

Crowley grinned. "Well, all right. So we're not noble soldiers of the cause." He paused and looked thoughtful. "I do insist that we do something for the general. He deserves a few comforts for his remaining years."

"Agreed."

Crowley grinned again. "Excellent. As his prospective son-in-law you can provide for him. Now, how much do *you* want."

"More than my share, naturally."

"It does appear that you earned a bonus in that battle. I'll consider it."

"You are most kind," Slocum said. But as he wrapped himself back into his blanket, he refrained from planning on how he would spend the money.

Slocum was nearly asleep when the next petitioner came to arouse him. Since neither was at ease in the other's language, they spoke Spanish.

"Did you find the pistols worked well for you?" Giraud asked.

"They worked perfectly," Slocum said. "Why don't you come to the point?"

"As you wish. How much did he offer you?"

"No specific figure was mentioned."

"Your gallantry of this afternoon should not go unrewarded."

Slocum wondered whatever had happened to the days when virtue was its own reward.

"I should say twenty percent more," Giraud mused.

"One hundred and twenty percent of nothing remains nothing," Slocum said. "It is curious how numbers play such tricks."

"Ah. What can I do to change your mind?"

"Come to the next point. My faith in the tooth fairy vanished early in sixty-four. Spell out what you want and what it is worth."

"For myself I seek nothing," Giraud said.

"I am pleased to hear that," Slocum said. "For that is easily arranged. Now perhaps I can sleep?"

"But my men have served and suffered."

"Do I hear violins?"

"Please. I do not play the noble hero. How much longer do you believe they will serve and suffer?"

"That," Slocum said, "puts an entirely different face upon the matter."

"Exactly. And if such thoughts cross their minds, it is a leader's duty to lead—"

"If he wishes to continue as leader."

"I see that you understand."

"Perfectly," Slocum assured him. "Of course, there remains the matter of General van Arnem. . . ."

Giraud sighed. "A great man in his day, but now quite mad. I should think there is enough for his honorable retirement—and that this is more of concern to his son-in-law?"

And that, Slocum thought, is pretty near the truth. "Another ten percent should ease his declining years."

"Excellent. We are agreed. So, when the moment of truth arrives, you will promise that I'm not forgotten."

"No gold, no promises," Slocum said.

"But I cannot give what I do not yet possess."

"Work at it awhile," Slocum said. "I'm sure you'll come up with a way."

"Perhaps."

After Giraud left, Slocum lay wrapped in his blanket, staring at the blaze of summer stars overhead, wondering exactly what was the secret of his sudden popularity. It wasn't as if this army of sixty men—well, more like fifty after the battle with the *juaristas*—needed him that badly. He had made no demands for a cut and had no realistic hopes of getting any. So what did they want from him?

The legionnaries clearly would follow Giraud as long as there was any hope of gain. Possibly beyond that. Habits die hard. They outgunned Crowley's Southerners two to one, and if they decided to take the gold, adding one Slocum to either side wouldn't much change those odds. So why did both Crowley and Giraud think they needed Slocum?

Slowly he began to guess. The day he and Joe had come up toward the Cross Seven, he had been surprised by one sentry while watching another search the trail with field glasses. It had been only seconds after Mojave Joe's disappearance. That second man must have seen Slocum traveling with an Indian—and now an Indian was spooking sentries with well-placed arrows. Slocum grinned up at the stars. God, wouldn't old Joe be delighted if he were here to share the joke! Those fifty men, Crowley, Giraud—they were scared spitless! They thought Slocum was going to take it all away from them. Slocum and all his wild Indians were going to steal the gold!

They probably thought he had Vásquez lined up to help, too!

He was still hard-pressed not to smile when they rode back into the Cross Seven spread a day later. It was mid-morning of still another brilliantly cloudless day, and there had not been the slightest hint of further trouble. The sentinels were all in place at the ranch.

They did not seem happy to see their returned comrades. Even shouted exaggerations of how much gold they had found got little beyond a grumpy "C'mon in" from the guards. Slocum wondered if there would be a fresh squabble, with still another faction complaining about an as-yet-theoretical division of the gold. Or had Mojave Joe been stirring things up here, too?

There was a new tent pitched over beyond the boars' nest. New recruits, Slocum supposed. He wondered how welcome they would be now that— But of course they would be welcome. Now private soldiers would be hiring flunkies to polish their boots, draw their water, hew their wood. Within a week the gold, no matter how liberally distributed, would end up concentrated among a prudent few.

Crowley and Giraud were still competing for his favor but growing increasingly puzzled as the party approached home without being attacked. Slocum struggled unsuccessfully to conceal his amusement, which only made them that much surer that his fangs were still undrawn. Extra guards were posted around the perimeter. Crowley and Giraud beckoned to Slocum, and the three of them went to report to General van Arnem.

Laura appeared in the doorway. "Man to see you," she said. It took Slocum a moment to realize that she was talking to him. He squinted, and it was Cavanaugh. It struck Slocum that this was one coincidence too many.

General van Arnem appeared, looking slightly more alert this morning. "Captain Crowley," he said. "Have you accomplished your errand?"

"In spades—sir." Crowley caught himself. Then he saw Cavanaugh.

But Cavanaugh was looking at Slocum. "You found it?"

Oh, my, Slocum thought. How the news does fly!

When nobody denied it, Cavanaugh stepped outside. Standing in the yard, he drew his revolver and fired twice into the air. There were .44-caliber replies on four sides of the camp. "I'm afraid you're all under arrest, gentlemen," Cavanaugh said.

"Just who the hell are you?" Crowley said.

Slocum didn't have to ask. Why hadn't he guessed

it from the long faces of those guards? It was hard to be cheerful with a gun trained on your back. "I fancy you'll discover he's a Pinkerton," he said.

There was a moment of startled silence while Crowley digested this. "So that's your game!" he finally snarled.

Slocum shook his head. "I fear we are equally victims," he explained. "I've met Mr. Cavanaugh before and been curious about the way he kept reappearing in my uninteresting life." Turning to Cavanaugh, he said, "You *are* a Pink, I presume."

The man nodded. "And that's the sheriff and something over one hundred of this county's citizens out there surrounding us, in case you have some idea of resistance."

"The gold is legitimate spoils of war," Crowley protested.

"And it's being despoiled again," Slocum said. "Who's taking it this time?"

"The United States Treasury," Cavanaugh said.

"And just what are we charged with?" Slocum demanded. "I hadn't heard that finding buried treasure was a crime."

Cavanaugh laughed. "Come now. Plotting rebellion against the United States is a fairly serious offense. And your companion there was certainly involved in piracy against a United States warship. General van Arnem is an escaped prisoner—"

"A prisoner convicted of nothing," Slocum said. "Damn you, Cavanaugh. I thought you were a pretty good man. I guess I had you wrong all the time."

"I lived through the war," Cavanaugh said. "I shouldn't want to live through another. That gold in the hands of Southern diehards is more dangerous than dynamite." His voice softened. "Without the gold I don't suppose that your people are such a threat. I expect that if you apply for a pardon, it will be granted with little difficulty. Now, order your men to lay down their arms."

"You abuse my hospitality, sir." It was General van Arnem, who looked as if he had just aroused himself from a midday nap.

Cavanaugh retained enough decency to be embarrassed. "My apologies, General. This seemed the only way to accomplish my mission without bloodshed. Now, once again, please ask your men to disarm themselves before the sheriff and his posse lose their patience."

"I must confer with my officers," van Arnem said. "Major Slocum, you will favor me with your estimate of the situation."

"Frankly, sir, we haven't a chance," Slocum said. "We're surrounded and outnumbered."

"Captain Crowley, do you concur?"

Reluctantly, Crowley nodded.

"Captain Giraud?"

"We will lose, *mon général*. But La Légion étrangére does not lightly surrender. At your command we can make these swine pay."

"Thank you," van Arnem said. "But I fear it would be pointless slaughter." He drew his sword and presented it hilt-first to Cavanaugh. "Your prisoner, sir."

The sheriff was sweating when he came in. "All right, Abe," he said. "The prisoners and the posse are all headed for town. We can load up the gold." He grinned at Cavanaugh. "Clean sweep, and without a fight. You did a good job, talking them into surrendering."

"Why were we not permitted to go with the others?" General van Arnem demanded.

The sheriff didn't answer. Slocum wondered that himself. Why keep him and Laura and the old general separated from the others? He saw certain obvious explanations, and did not like what he concluded. "Really thought better of you than that," he told Cavanaugh. "But I should've remembered you're a Yankee."

"Were all Southerners gentlemen?" Cavanaugh asked. "I don't recall Quantrill being on our side."

Slocum shrugged. "If we'd won, I wonder if we'd still be locking up old men years after it was over."

"Makes no never-mind," the sheriff growled. To

Cavanaugh he added, "Better lock them Southern gentlemen up. We're gonna be busy for a while."

Cavanaugh seemed puzzled, but he dutifully produced handcuffs and leg irons. With the sheriff and Abe both watching closely, there was no way to resist, and Slocum found himself shackled. Cavanaugh brushed past where Laura was sitting and reached for General van Arnem.

"You cur!" The old man snapped from his chair with surprising speed and thrust his cane saberlike at the Pinkerton. There came a boom that was ear-shattering inside the small cabin, and the old man abruptly sat back in his chair, eyes vacant with surprise and outrage. He continued sagging until he keeled over and out of the chair and landed on the mudsill floor. In death he was surprisingly small.

Cavanaugh spun to stare at the sheriff, who held a smoking Colt. "My God," he said gasping. "You didn't have to do that!"

"Like hell I didn't," the sheriff replied, and shot Cavanaugh.

The sheriff stepped over Cavanaugh and grabbed Laura by the wrist. Eyes blank and unseeing, she allowed herself to be led outside.

Slocum raged helplessly. He knew he should have killed Sheriff Bigelow when he had the chance. Now there wasn't likely to be another.

XV

Cavanaugh's stare was unfocused, but Slocum got an excellent view of the sheriff's men who trooped in and out of the house loading packhorses with a half million dollars in gold—at sixteen real, redeemable-in-specie dollars per ounce, very nearly one ton. They were planning on traveling far and fast, Slocum knew, for they had divided the gold into twenty separate loads. There were nine men, counting the sheriff. They would take remounts, and that would just about wipe out the remnant of the Cross Seven remuda. What difference did it make? They were letting Slocum see their faces. He wondered why they had not killed him already. Could he possibly have anything else they could want or use?

The sheriff's hand-picked men all seemed to bear some faint family resemblance to that solid, red-mustached horse killer. But he had heard one called Higgins and another Bryant. A Luke and a Moe were among them, too, but except for Abe, he had not connected any of the red, beefy faces with names. Cavanaugh heaved a tremendous, racking sigh and immediately started bleeding.

Slocum was startled. He'd thought the Pinkerton agent was dead. Soon would be, the way that blood was seeping out of a punctured lung. Slocum had seen this final rally of a dying man before; once had even seen a battlefield funeral service interrupted in an unforgettable manner. The detective's head rolled, and his eyes fixed on Slocum. "Sorry," he managed.

So was Slocum.

One of the sheriff's men came in and picked up the final hundred pounds of gold.

"Abe, God damn it, will you git smart about it!" somebody called from outside. The sandy-haired man hurried out without a glance at Slocum or Cavanaugh. Wind blew the door shut behind him. Then, as he heard a bar drop, Slocum knew it had not been the wind. He glanced at the general, who seemed to have sprawled out to sleep beside his chair. It would be hard to say whether it was the bullet or this final outrage that had killed the old man. But at least he was dead. He was not like Slocum: shackled hand and foot in a locked house and smelling smoke.

"Sorry." It was Cavanaugh again. "Key in my pocket."

A lot of good that would do Slocum, his hands shackled behind him. He could see flames licking at the door now, smoke oozing around its edges. In half a minute the dry-stick cabin would explode. He knelt off his chair and squirmed, trying to put his back to Cavanaugh. The Pink was trying. He was also dying. Flames grew, and Slocum knew they had tossed a torch up onto the roof as well. He felt Cavanaugh scrabbling feebly at the handcuffs. It felt like hands. There was no metal-on-metal sound of a key. All he could hear was the growing roar of fire.

Now nothing at all was happening behind him. Cavanaugh had managed to up and die on him. Which pocket? How long would it take him to rummage through an inert body's various coat and trouser pockets with his hands shackled behind him? More time than it would take for this cabin to cremate him. Already the heat and smoke lay so low that Slocum was having trouble breathing down on the mudsill floor. He felt blindly behind him, and there was a tiny metal-on-metal sensation. By God, Cavanaugh was still trying! A moment later the shackle on one of Slocum's hands loosened.

He spun and captured the key, praying the same key would fit his leg irons. It did. With cuffs dangling from his left wrist, he crawled on his belly toward the door. It was barred. Abruptly he remembered Cavanaugh, but when he looked this time, the Pinkerton was most definitely dead. Slocum suspected he was, too, but just hadn't discovered it yet.

There were a pair of scraped-rabbit-skin windows

on opposite ends of the cabin, but he knew he would never be able to crawl through either of those tiny openings. He picked up the heavy handmade chair in which General van Arnem had died. Bending low as he could to avoid the heat and the mephitic air, he charged the door.

There was little hope of breaking down the door even after a good scorching, but, as Slocum had prayed, the grease-soaked rawhide hinges had consumed themselves faster than the door's planking. The top half of the door burst outward and the bottom half swiveled inward, pivoting around the bar. Slocum rolled up and over and landed running. Twenty feet away he could barely endure the heat of the flames.

The sheriff and his gang had departed. Laura was gone, too, and so were all the horses. Somebody had gone through the surrendered weapons and smashed all those he hadn't thought worth carrying away. Three worn but usable repeating rifles had been bent around tree trunks. What was steel when there was gold to carry? But they had run out of time. Several pistols were still in working order, including Slocum's own. Why destroy a dead man's weapons?

But the ruined weapons told their own story. The sheriff expected the posse to return, and it wouldn't do to leave weapons for Cross Seven troops, who would, Slocum suspected, be part of the posse when the citizens found out just what their honorable Sheriff Bigelow had done.

The cabin was still burning furiously. He sighed. At least he wouldn't have to worry about what to do with the general's and the Pinkerton's remains. What was he going to do with his own? What was he going to do about Laura? He remembered how short he had been with her. But that had been when he faced imminent death and she did not. Now . . . He shuddered, remembering what the Indians had done to her. If the same were to happen again, only this time at the hands of white men . . .

He had to trail them, catch up somehow, and fast. Which meant he needed weapons, food, horses. They had fired the cabin, but the boars' nest still stood. He went to it and began rummaging about, picking up a few ounces of powder from one man's bindle, a handful of pistol balls from another. Finally he had enough for his Colts.

He went back to the arms pile and stared in dismay. There were no useful rifles. The pistols would have to do.

He had weapons, but no horse. He'd have to follow on foot. The sheriff's gang would not be able to move as fast as a man alone, but a pack train limited to one hundred pounds per beast could move out right smart, and they were already at least one half hour ahead of him. Where in the hell was he going to get a horse?

Clank! The arrow struck the brass sheathing on a rifle stock, and flint shattered. Slocum looked behind him in time to see a grinning, wrinkled face he had not expected to see again.

"God damn it, Joe, will you stop playing around!"

The Indian's face registered sudden surprise. "You bet. God damn. I see your horse go." Mojave Joe pointed east. "What you do here?"

"What're you doing here?"

The old Indian grinned. "Big place. Man go. Get food, get gun."

"You won't find any that work here," Slocum warned. "I don't know about food."

Joe rubbed his belly. "Been cook house. Find gun, too." He displayed a pistol.

Abruptly Slocum realized how long it had been since last he had taken on stores. He would not be helping Laura by starving himself. He went around to the ramada that served as kitchen and began feeding himself from the bread and leftover stew that was still just this side of sour. By the time he had eaten, the cabin was a pile of smoking ashes.

"See any horses around here?" Slocum asked.

"You bet."

"I mean now, after they're all gone."

Joe had not.

"Those rascals stole my woman. I need a horse so I can go steal her back."

"What they carry all them horse?"

"Gold." Abruptly, Slocum realized he might have a possible ally. "Any way we can find Tiburcio Vásquez? There's enough gold out there to keep him happy for years."

"No. Vásquez all ride north. Go steal 'nother town for a while."

Slocum didn't think he had scared them that bad. Must have been planning it beforehand. But it left him alone and unhorsed while that Yankee-bastard sheriff and his men got off with Laura and the gold. He could have made a deal with Vásquez: gold for you, girl for me.

"Joe, you owe me something."

"You bet."

"I need a horse."

"You bet."

"Can you get me a good one?"

"You bet."

You better, Slocum thought. Or my name's Mudd. His head ached. He stared downhill, in the direction the sheriff had gone. What would this do to Laura? First Indians, then her father. And what were those motherless bastards doing to her?

Nothing right now, he consoled himself. They were heading east, making tracks. Laura would be safe at least until they made camp. After that . . . He didn't want to think about that. "Joe, do you still have that—" He looked around, but Mojave Joe was gone.

He tried to take stock. It was still only midafternoon. He walked the perimeter of the camp, praying somebody might have overlooked a horse. No such luck. Crowley's and Giraud's men had taken the entire remuda with them when they went for the gold, and there had not been time to put them out to pasture before the sheriff's posse moved in from all four sides. With the horses still tied, there had been no strays. He wondered what those solid citizens were thinking now that they had retired to town with fifty men guilty of no crime—and now neither evidence nor sheriff nor the Pinkerton who'd enlisted them. Chances were they would hang all the Cross Seven men. They'd about have to. There was no way to jail them, and those old soldiers would have long memories.

Slocum walked aimlessly, kicking horse biscuits and reexamining his Colts. They seemed no worse for having been tossed atop the pile of ruined weapons. The sheriff had been in a hurry and knew there was no danger of a shackled and cremated Slocum's ever making his way as far as the arms pile.

There was nothing to do. Joe had gone for horses, and it made no sense to set out without him.

There was one thing he could do, though. He could give a decent burial to whatever he could find of the general and Cavanaugh. He began looking for a shovel.

A crow cawed.

Not again! Slocum dodged behind a tree and patted his Colts. Then he saw a pair of crows squabbling in the top of a sugar pine. Nerves, he guessed. Something fell from the squabbling crows. He saw what it was, then redoubled his efforts to find a shovel.

He found one by the latrine trenches. He had not dug half deep enough before he saw the irony of his daydreams of buying a ranch and settling down to an honest life with Laura. He studied his swollen, blistered hands. Good God, did farming and ranching people do this kind of thing day after day? He had been a soldier too long. It would be days before he could properly handle a deck of cards again.

If she was alive. If he could get her back. What would they do? The only things he had done in his adult life were fight and gamble. Could he be a lawman? He couldn't do any worse a job of it than the sheriff of San Bernardino.

Finally the grave was dug. He raked the ashes and got two things that had once been a detective and a general into a blanket. Afterward he sat with blistered hands around his knees and stared toward the east. The way they had taken Laura.

Slocum aroused with a jerk. Somewhere in the darkness a horse had blown. He cupped hands before his ears and turned slowly, trying to locate the sound. It sounded like more than one horse. Then abruptly he saw them: two horses being led. But who was doing the leading? There was nobody riding them. No pack saddles either.

"Hey, God damn, you bet!"

"Over here," Slocum said. "Where'd you get them?"

"Crazy sumbitch."

Slocum thought Mojave Joe was addressing him until the Indian went on in his fractured way to explain the chaos that had developed along the trail back to San Bernardino. Slocum figured some leveler heads among the townspeople must have begun to wonder just what charges could be laid against the Cross Seven riders—and what countercharges and suits could erode their own carefully accumulated earnings. There had been a noisy meeting along the trail, according to Joe. It must have become obvious that they were not being caught up with by either sheriff or gold. By now it seemed likely both townspeople and Cross Seven people were in alliance and searching for their betrayers.

"And in the midst of this you didn't just steal a couple of horses," Slocum marveled, "you got my own Dorkus back!"

"You bet." Joe was cheerful.

"But why weren't you riding?"

"Easy walk. Faster, too. Horse only good for eat. Don't know why you want 'em."

"Tools," Slocum explained. "Weapons. I'm going to use these horses to kill about nine men."

"White men?"

"Yup."

"God damn! You bet. You killum fast?"

"Don't believe I will."

"Le's go."

By dawn Mojave Joe was ready to concede that horses were sometimes useful for matters other than eating, but he still would not sit Slocum's remount for more than a mile before sliding off to go trotting pigeon-toed ahead of the two horses. "You're sure they came this way?" Slocum asked. There were so many hoofprints from the going and coming of the gold-seeking expedition that he could not see in the darkness.

But Mojave Joe's ancient eyes seemingly had no problem analyzing the mass of hoof marks that went one way, then the other way on top of old ones. To him the third set of tracks heading back east was as obvious as the "Follow me" carved into a Greek whore's sandals.

Just as the sun was breaking free, the sheriff's tracks turned away from the main trail and began angling down a steep canyon toward the desert floor. Slocum dismounted and stood beside Mojave Joe. "Any idea of where he's heading?"

The Indian shrugged. "Go 'cross desert. Crazy sumbitch."

"Can it be done?"

"I go. But I no carry horse. White man only cross desert winter."

"Where will he cross the river?"

"Needles? Blythe? How the hell I know?"

"How far ahead of us are they?"

"You smell." Joe held horse dung up to Slocum's face. It could not be more than a couple hours old.

"Let's go," Slocum said.

"Like hell. I walk yesterday. I run, catch horse last night. I walk this night. Mojave Joe sleep now."

"But we've got to catch them—"

"You already crazy. Go in sun like this, what good you do for woman? Joe sleep now."

Slocum saw the tiredness behind that perpetual grin. He reminded himself that this Indian was the "oldest man in the world." And Joe was right; Slocum was staggering tired already. What good would it do to catch the sheriff if he couldn't do anything. He looked out across the desert and shuddered. Joe knew the desert. With Mojave Joe's help Slocum had a chance. Without it . . .

"All right," Slocum said. "I'm feelin' a bit tuckered, too."

The sun was offering a foretaste of hell before they had hobbled and nose-bagged the horses. They found a notch between a pair of massive boulders and squeezed in. Slocum prayed it would not seem as cool and attractive to the rattlers as it did to him and curled up in the shade.

He was utterly exhausted, but sleep would not come. How was Laura taking this? And why had the sheriff chosen to cross the desert in midsummer? Where was he going?

The thoughts crowded his head and drove off sleep. The sheriff couldn't go toward the coast. The telegraph was faster than any man could travel, and it wouldn't be long before every lawman—and every bounty hunter—in California would be looking for Bigelow and his gold.

But why the desert? Did Vásquez figure in this? It seemed to Slocum that Vásquez owned everything the California Rangers didn't. Vásquez. He'd been polite. He didn't kill for the fun of it. Would he help? Didn't matter. If Mojave Joe couldn't find Vásquez, Slocum sure as hell couldn't.

The sheriff was crossing the desert. He had to be making for the river. Which way would he turn? South toward Mexico, or north to Nevada, where it would be easy to remelt the gold and bring it out as newly mined?

He had given up all thought of sleep when it came, suddenly.

When he woke, amid nightmares of burning houses, the sun had angled around, and he was so hot that for a moment he saw double. He prodded Joe, and the Indian crawled blearily out of the concentrated sunlight.

"God damn," Joe grumbled.

They found shade behind another rock, but this one had spent the first half of the day warming, and the heat was nigh unbearable. Slocum looked downhill. They were only halfway down the slope that tilted from snow to salt flat. He wondered if the sheriff and his companions had found shelter. And Laura? He reminded himself that she had spent years in rough country. And at least she knew how to ride. But they had the gold. There was only one reason for them to take an attractive young woman along. Would she be too sore to ride already?

The horses had crowded behind a house-sized boulder where they stood head to tail, as horses are wont to do, using one another's tails to keep flies from their faces. Slocum was not happy about the angle at which their heads drooped. How many days of this could a horse stand?

Too bad American horses couldn't learn to endure the smell of camels. Back before the Confederacy, one of Jefferson Davis's pet projects in the War Department had been a camel corps. But camels were ill-tempered. They stank. They bit. Men hated them, and horses would not live in the same camp with them. What was required for this country, Slocum suspected, was some sort of steam engine that did not require tracks. Put wide wheels on it so it would not sink into the sand. Rig some kind of condenser to reduce boiler-water consumption. . . . He sighed. It would never work.

"What are we waiting for?" Slocum demanded. "Let's go!"

Mojave Joe struggled for words. "They ride in this, we no ride, we catch 'em sooner. You bet."

"And if they're not riding now?" Slocum asked.

Joe shrugged. "You want go in desert with dead horse? Man live in desert longer than horse. Those men carry something heavy. They never carry without horses. You bet. I tell you when time we go. You bet."

Reluctantly Slocum found shade again. The heat bore down like a weight. He willed time to pass, but the sun didn't seem to move. "Damn it, I can't just sit here!" he shouted.

Joe shrugged. "Le's go."

Slocum's eyes came back into focus, and abruptly he was seeing what he had been looking at ever since Joe came back with the horses. "You brought the buffalo gun!"

"You bet. Le's go."

There were still three hours of sunlight when they started down the canyon. An hour later they reached the desert floor. Slocum had thought the foothills were hot. On the desert itself was more than heat. The world shimmered as far as he could see, and the air was so hot that he hated to breathe.

They rode in silence. Slocum's pulse pounded at his temples. He'd heard of men going mad in the desert. Would he? Would Laura? Had the sheriff lost his mind?

There were no tracks that Slocum could see. In his stint with the cavalry he'd learned to read sign, but that was on the grassy Texas plains. This burning waste of alkali dust and low scrub held marks only until the dry wind covered them with dust and sand. Joe walked ahead, eyes on the ground. Sometimes he stopped and blew at dust until hoofprints showed. Then he walked on.

The world had shrunk to an infinity of dust and heat; hot, dry wind, and always the dust. . . .

"What's buffalo?" Mojave Joe asked suddenly.

Slocum coughed. His mouth was dry and it was hard to talk. "I told you. It's like a big cow. But wild."

"Man shoot 'em?"

"Do they ever! Keep it up the way they're goin' and one of these days they're going to start running short of free meat and hides."

"Eat 'em?"

"Yes. Tastes just like a cow."

Joe made a face. "No good," he said. "Eat cow, be cow. Eat horse, run fast. East *tigre,* man strong. Eat *burro,* man smart."

That didn't make sense, but Slocum knew there was a difference between Indians who ate buffalo and those who ate reservation beef. "How far ahead are they now?" he asked.

"How the hell I know?" They rode on. The sun fell behind faraway mountains to the west, but the twilight lingered. The desert cooled slowly. Finally Joe sniffed crushed *pitahaya* stalks and said, "Maybe two hour."

XVI

"How you shoot 'em?"

Joe was still curious about the huge buffalo gun.

"Well, you understand what the monopod's for, don't you?"

"You say?"

"That leg up near the muzzle." When the Indian still looked blank, Slocum swung it into place. "Make'm stand still," he explained. "And that brass thing on top is a telescope sight. Hold it up and look through it."

The Indian raised the lengthy weapon and squinted through the brass scope, extending a tongue from the corner of his mouth as he struggled to keep his other eye shut. "Sumbitch!" he said, and almost dropped the rifle.

"What is it?"

Mojave Joe was still squinting ahead where he had pointed the rifle.

"See 'em. Then he go 'way."

Slocum halted his gelding and dismounted. "Let's see."

"Maybe better you not look," Joe said.

"Why?"

Joe shrugged. He made no resistance when Slocum took the rifle.

John squinted through the telescope. It had more light-gathering power than he had suspected; in fact, it was almost a night glass. He swept the velvety, moonless night by the light of brilliant stars and was startled by a glimpse of hell.

The image was blurred, and it was impossible to hold it steady. Slocum growled low in his throat.

The sheriff had made camp in the scant shade of an ocotillo. Men lounged at varying distances to watch the show. One man lay naked on his back atop a blanket. His knees were flexed, and he was huffing mightily with the effort of his thrusting.

Laura's naked, sunburned body draped limply atop him, and for an instant Slocum thought she was dead. He strained to hold the rifle steady, and saw there was tiny spark of life remaining in her twitching body. Her arms lay limp on each side of the man beneath her. Her thighs were spread wide to accommodate his insatiable plunging. Her full, firm breasts were mashed against his hairy chest.

And on top, pressing Laura's female flesh in this lustful sandwich, the three-hundred-pound horse killer of a sheriff was thrusting his manhood into her ass, driving hard against her sprawled body. With each thrust into her the sheriff was flattening her, squeezing the breath from her until the girl no longer breathed, only gasped in automatic reaction each time the pressure on her rib cage was momentarily relaxed.

And the others were laughing. Slocum could see their thigh-slapping mirth.

He wondered if he had gone mad. He stared in horror and disgust and was sickened to feel his own manhood stretching his trousers.

Slocum drew a deep, shuddering breath and cocked the buffalo gun. The light was terrible and the range too far, and Laura was in the middle. He knew it was impossible, but he had to do something. It would have been a kindness to kill her.

He aimed for the sheriff's broad back and began to squeeze the trigger, hesitated a moment, and raised the aim point. Then he squeezed off the round.

The hammer snapped down on an empty nipple. The rifle was empty. He hadn't tried to fire an empty rifle in twenty years.

Slocum cursed and drew a pistol, but even as he did, he knew it was hopeless. He couldn't even see them without the telescope.

They were all watching the show. Could he ride up and take them now?

That idea was insane, but Slocum couldn't think straight, not with hate for the sheriff and horror at what he had seen and disgust with himself boiling inside his skull like disturbed fire ants. He grabbed powder and ball, scattering supplies, losing a handful of caps in the dark, frantic in his haste to load the rifle. Carefully, he told himself. Do it right. You get only one shot. He forced his hands to work slowly.

When he looked again, the sheriff was gone, and so was the man who had been beneath her. Two other strangers were dabbing at Laura's inert nakedness with a wadded-up shirt. A third was taking off his pants.

Slocum aimed, and this time he was able to will his body to icy stillness. He took a deep breath, let off half, squeezed off the round. The big rifle crashed, its sound echoing off some distant hill.

The man he'd aimed at was pulling up his pants, and the others were running frantically. Two grabbed Laura and pulled her away, out of Slocum's sight. Again he went through the frantic motions of reloading, but when the rifle was ready, he saw that they had broken camp and were moving out.

Slocum had not known such sickening anger since the last time he had wept—when the news came from Appomattox. But though his rage brought him to the edge of nausea, his voice was steady. "I will kill them," he promised. "All of them." He turned to Joe. "But if you want any of them, I give you my blessing. Just let them die slowly."

"Eatum liver," Joe said. "Good for eyes. Good for teeth. You bet."

"Can you eat a man's liver while he's alive enough to watch you do it?" Slocum asked.

Mojave Joe was shocked. "God damn. I don' know. Never try. You want eat 'em, first we got catch 'em. You bet."

"Indeed. Let's go." They mounted and moved rapidly toward the sheriff's camp. Slocum was not surprised to find the site empty.

More hours passed as the horses stumbled through a moonless night. Gradually, weariness replaced the frustrated rage that Slocum had felt. Would he ever catch them? Now that they were warned—

Joe moved ahead more cautiously now. Slocum wondered if he were riding into ambush. Would the sheriff take the time? Probably not. The real enemy was the desert, far more dangerous to the sheriff than a following posse.

Why the hell did I warn them? Slocum thought. So, Laura was raped. She's been raped before, and she'll be raped again before I get close enough to do any good. I could have moved closer. . . .

Had he gone mad already? Between the heat and the vision of madness he had seen, his brain boiled with confused thoughts, and he could think of nothing beyond killing the sheriff and all his men. Maybe I have gone mad, he thought. I've got to start thinking straight, or I'll be no damned good to anybody.

Mojave Joe dropped back. "Quiet now," he warned.

Even as the old Indian spoke, Dorkus's ears swiveled forward. Slocum reined to a halt and jumped down to grasp the gelding by the mouth before it could give away his position.

"God damn," Joe whispered. "Killum. Eatum liver. You bet."

"Not my Dorkus, you don't," Slocum said. "Hold his mouth. Like this." He reached for the other horse. "That will keep them quiet."

"This, too," Joe said. He touched a knife at his belt. But he held the horses while Slocum took out the buffalo rifle and set the monopod. He stared into starlight, and sure as death in Texas, there ahead was another horse.

It was at least a couple of miles ahead. Slocum squinted around, trying to look slightly off center and still see through the telescope, but it was no use. He folded up the monopod.

A mile ahead was a darker patch that might be vegetation. He put finger to lips and they began walking the horses toward it. Mojave Joe was struggling with his mount. "How you make goddamn horse be still?" he hissed.

Slocum knew he had made a mistake. Perhaps the Indian was right about horses being good only for food. But he hoped he would never have to live long without one. The only thing Slocum really feared in life was being left afoot—that and a good woman. "Take the horses back a ways," he said.

"You take'm."

It was no time to argue. Left to his own devices, Joe might settle for a mouthful of fresh horse liver. Slocum began leading the horses back. Two hundred yards behind, he tied them to a clump of greasewood and hoped the faint drift of desert air would not betray him with a fresh scent of strange horse.

"God damn!" Joe said as John approached awhile later.

Even though he had been expecting it, the whispered greeting startled Slocum. "How many men?" he asked.

"Two. Man come. Other man go to sleep."

So Joe had witnessed the changing of the guard. Confident lot of bastards. Did they actually believe he wouldn't follow them? Slocum sensed that Mojave Joe had something more to say.

"They talk," Joe said.

"Oh?"

"They talk lot."

"About what?"

Joe seemed embarrassed. "They talk 'bout do to woman. Sumbitch bad men. You bet."

Slocum got control of himself. "How far's the main camp?"

" 'Nother mile."

"And I suppose the guard went back there to sleep, leaving one man out here alone on watch."

Joe puzzled over this for a moment, then brightened. "You bet. One man."

Slocum sighed. Everything had to start somewhere. "Wait here," he said.

"Le's go."

"No. If I don't come back, have all the fun you want with the others. Kill the girl if you can do it clean and quick. I don't care how much you hurt the men."

"Le's go."

"No, damn it! I don't want us both caught. Besides, somebody's got to look after the horses."

"Eat 'em," Joe promised.

"Come to think of it," Slocum added, "there's going to be quite a price on those men sooner or later. If they get me, you can sell them to the warden or the sheriff at Yuma."

"You bet!"

"Back in an hour," Slocum said, and started walking through darkness.

Up ahead he could not see very well, but there was enough starlight to avoid major obstacles. If he looked slightly to one side he could, with some effort, make things out. Somewhere ahead he heard bridle hardware jingle as a horse tossed its head. He stepped out —and fell straight down into nothingness.

Slocum was so startled he would have yelled if he'd had the wind. But even though the ground beneath him was soft, the breath was completely knocked out of him. He lay gasping, struggling not to make any more noise than he already had. Where in hell was he? Canyons, tunnels, in the desert? He rolled over and saw starlight. He lay in the bottom of some sort of trench. The sides were vertical and too new for erosion. He stood, and his head was still below the level of the surrounding plain. After a moment he decided he had not broken anything.

He began walking, knowing any trench like this would be the logical gathering place for every sidewinder within miles. He walked nearly a quarter of a mile before the trench became shallow enough for him to scramble out without creating a rockslide.

He stood in the darkness and tried to work out where he was. Then abruptly he heard the horse blow again. It sounded practically on top of him. But it took another ten minutes of cautious blundering before he actually saw the beast. There was no man on it.

Not tending to business, Slocum decided. The rider had spent enough time in the saddle for one day. He would be hunkered down somewhere near his horse.

Probably sentry duty was as perfunctory as it could be to men sure they were not being pursued.

Slocum studied the sky. He searched for the Big Dipper with some difficulty, since the sky was almost too brilliantly full of stars to pick out any single constellation. Finally he found it and began a pussyfooting, square search about the horse that stood breathing noisily. The poor beast, Slocum reflected, did not know what was in store for it before it would cross this desert and attain steamy, muddy refuge at the Colorado, where cattails and cactus joined improbably.

On the third leg of his square, and treading cautiously lest he fall into the trench again, Slocum finally saw the rider. It was the sandy-haired one, Abe, who'd stood guard with Cavanaugh and laughed when the Pinkerton mentioned a jury. This bastard had certainly known what the sheriff intended.

He'd also been the man who barred the cabin door.

I'm the only judge and jury here, Slocum thought. And the verdict is guilty.

He began gently walking up behind the sitting man. No point in creeping, which would merely put him closer to the ground, the heat, the snakes, and possibly make him bump into some noise maker he would not encounter striding at full height. But, damn, it was dark! He stepped cautiously and greasewood snapped.

The sentry was smart enough not to jump to his feet. Instead, he sat motionless. Slocum cursed the providence that could just as easily have made him step on that dry greasewood a mile away, where the noise would have made no difference. Too late now. He didn't want this to turn into a shooting match that would bring them all back out here. "Abe?" he said in a soft voice.

The tension went out of the hunched figure. "Goldang it, you hadn't ought to come sneakin' up on a feller like that."

"Muh horse's throwed a shoe. Tha's why I'm walkin'."

"Who is it? Man can't see diddly out here."

Slocum ignored the question until he got closer. The one called Abe still twisted his head as he peered into darkness. Slocum was coming up noiselessly behind him. He drew the Colt. He brought it down, laying the barrel smartly across Abe's sandy hair.

"Was she a good piece?" Slocum asked when a hog-tied Abe moved again.

"They 'uz all doin' it," the sandy-haired one said defensively.

"Then if God sees fit to endow me with the strength, they'll all get what you're going to."

"What you gonna do?"

"Surely you know what happens to rapists." Before Abe could offer more excuses, Slocum stuffed the man's shirt into his mouth and tied it with torn strips of the same. "Must've done something like this to *her,* didn't you. Or was it more amusing to listen to her?" Slocum cocked his left-hand Colt and surreptitiously rotated the cylinder until the open hammer lay poised over an empty chamber. Then, with the muzzle nuzzling Abe's ear, he drew his clasp knife and performed that barbarous surgery that is so much a part of the cattle business.

Abe squirmed and emitted shrill, inarticulate moans through the gag. Halfway through the operation Abe managed a great straining lunge that predictably forced Slocum's left forefinger to contract the trigger. In the shocked aftermath of the man's realization that there was not going to be any quick, easy way out of this, Slocum finished his surgery. It had been bloodier than he had expected. He tore another piece of the bandit's shirt and stuffed it into his crotch.

"Can't have you bleeding to death," he said. "I want you to live for at least a week. Preferably longer."

Abe spat out the gag and screamed. His cry echoed over the desert. From far away Slocum heard someone call.

"You've managed to warn your friends," Slocum said. "Now, we can't have you shooting at anybody for a while, can we?" Slocum wiped blood from his clasp knife and severed both index fingers at the first joint.

Abe screamed again. Slocum cut his hands loose.

"You know," he said, "I considered cutting your tongue out, too, but I'm a firm believer in the value of advertising. You *will* recommend me to your friends, won't you? They should get here soon." Slocum tipped his hat and wiped his knife clean again, then slipped into the desert to catch Abe's horse. The animal shied away from him, but Slocum managed to catch the bridle.

He waited until he heard others approaching Abe, and heard their cries of horror. Then he gave a rebel yell. As he went back to where he had left Joe and the horses, he felt his pulse pounding along the old saber scar.

There was blood over his hands and shirtsleeves, and Colorado River water was more than a hundred very dry miles away. Slocum rode up to Mojave Joe and dismounted.

The wrinkled Indian was shocked. "You crazy sum-bitch!" he said when he saw Slocum's bloody sleeves.

Slocum considered this. Joe's diagnosis was probably correct. Jesus! What had he done? He could never plead "spur of the moment" for all the blood on his hands. Slocum had gone toward that sentry with malice aforethought.

The captured horse had a canteen on the saddle horn, but there would be better uses for water than washing. Even if he were to get the blood off his hands, Slocum knew he would never get it off his soul. He had passed a milestone that would forever set him apart from other men. He passed a blood-smeared hand over his forehead and wondered if he was imagining a mark there already. What shape was the mark of Cain? Did it look like a saber scar?

But Slocum knew. He had seen it in the last years of the war, in Mexico, and on the plains, wherever professionals had managed to master the art of killing without qualm. He remembered the first time he had killed a man, how drained and empty he had been for days afterward. He had been filled with strange thoughts of retreat into a monastery or God only knew what other nonsense. It was these post mortem letdowns that betrayed many professional *pistoleros*. After a big-killing high, there was always the letdown.

Slocum knew he was past redemption. How could he ever have entertained silly notions of settling down to a quiet life with Laura, with children? How, indeed, when he had known all his life, however obscurely, that this devil lurked within him? Slocum knew he was past redemption because bloody hands, post mortem letdown, and all, he was already scheming how to mangle the next one.

Had he made a tactical error leaving the man a tongue? He thought not. That they had an enemy trailing them would be obvious enough. It would help stretch their nerves to know it was Slocum. And if they talked enough about it, for poor Laura to hear it might even give her the nerve to endure for a few more days. But, Thundering Thursday, he had forgotten that they held a hostage for his good conduct. What would they do to her now?

Across from him in the starlight Mojave Joe squatted, eyes noncommittal in his wrinkled face. One of these two men was a savage.

"You crazy sumbitch," Joe repeated. "But one time I got trouble Yuma wife." He reached out to touch Slocum's blood-caked hands. Even in starlight, age and sorrow showed through that perpetual grin. Slocum was touched and embarrassed.

"Say, Joe, who's digging ditches in the middle of the desert?"

"Ditch come. Ditch go."

"What do you mean?"

Joe shrugged.

"Nothing just happens," Slocum insisted. "Is it a river or something?"

"One day got ditch. One day got hill." Joe mumbled something about Ometecutli, whom Slocum had met before as father of all the gods.

"You mean the ground just moves by itself?"

"You bet. Sometime knocks man down. Sometime man fall in, never see again."

Slocum had heard of earthquakes, but he'd never seen one. He hoped he wouldn't now.

"Le's go," the Indian said.

Slocum was more than ready. "But I don't want to get too close to those bastards."

"Hot tomorrow. Kill horse. Go now. Go round and get nex' water first."

"Is there a water hole ahead?"

" 'Bout twenty mile. Le's go."

Everyone had assured Slocum there was no water between here and the river. "You're sure?"

"Plenty water you, me. Horse—don' know. Maybe eat 'em."

"Not my gelding, you don't!" But Slocum understood that it might come to that. At least he had another horse now, and one more canteen of water. He would ride the bandit's horse tonight and spare Dorkus. If he had a brain in his head or an ounce of compassion in his soul, he would turn the poor beast loose and point it back toward the mountains, where there was water and graze. But he did not.

They mounted, leading the gelding. After a few minutes of riding, Joe slipped off his horse and reverted to walking. Slocum tried to turn his mind off and settle down to the rhythm of plodding horse. But he could no more forget what he had done than he could undo it. An hour passed, and if he was reading the angle of the Dipper handle correctly, they would be facing the sun before another two or three. "Suppose those rascals are up and on their way yet?" he wondered aloud.

"No talk," Joe hissed.

XVII

Slocum hadn't realized they were that close.

They rode another hour while he worked some calculations. Ten miles per hour on a good horse meant only fifteen hours to cover one hundred and fifty miles. Cutting down to six and one quarter miles per hour, which was about what infantry could do at double time, it would still take only twenty-four hours to make the distance from here to the Colorado's abundance of warm, muddy water. But if figures do not lie, then liars must figure. He wondered why the sheriff, who presumably knew this country, would even consider trying to get across the Mojave in summer. Probably because the desert was the only place they'd never think of looking. And the sheriff must have experience out here, good reason to think he could make it across.

He wished again for a camel. Whatever had happened to Jeff Davis's camel corps? The last Slocum knew, the camels had been turned loose. They'd probably all been eaten by Indians long ago. Their Islamic-Turkish-Greek drivers had married into Sonoran and Tucson families and were busy producing future presidents, some of whom had helped hound Slocum and his fellow legionnaires right out of the country.

What was that dastardly gold-stealing rapist of a sheriff up to? It would have made more sense for him to light a shuck for San Francisco, or San Pedro, San Diego—any of the ports where he might have caught a ship and gone where neither telegraph nor God's wrath could recall him to justice. Why head east through this branch office of hell?

Slocum concluded that the sheriff knew something he didn't. Certainly there were telegraph lines to the seaports. Maybe California's central valleys were closed to the sheriff, too. Slocum was used to the vast, uninhabited plains of Texas and New Mexico, but he had heard that central California was cut up into farms and ranches, as thickly populated as Illinois or Iowa.

But why was the sheriff so careless about guards? Possibly he wasn't being careless. They had searched what they thought was rifle range; they had been startled by his shot but not panicked. When they didn't find anyone within rifle range, they probably concluded that some stray desert rat had fired to warn them off his patch of the Mojave.

Which meant that Slocum knew something the sheriff didn't. Chances were that none of these men had ever hunted buffalo, that they had never seen a buffalo rifle. It wouldn't occur to any of them that a rifle could knock off a man's head from a mile or more away. They'd keep watch close at hand, but they couldn't be guarding out that far. If he stayed a mile behind and kept off the skyline, he could kill more before they understood the nature of his weapon.

But if the sheriff got away from Slocum, could he escape his other pursuers?

The government had locked up poor old General van Arnem for seven years and been ready to lock him up for seven more. They weren't going to give up now. And the Pinkertons had a man to avenge. If that wasn't enough, there were the *juaristas*. Jesus! Even Slocum was on the sheriff's golden tail. Where did the man plan on going?

The sheriff would, Slocum concluded, be delighted at the way somebody was doing his dirty work for him. It had taken so many men and so many horses to mount an expedition like this. If Slocum would just keep picking them off one at a time as supplies and water were used up, the remainder of the company would get through in fine shape—and with fewer shares to distribute. He was going to have to change his tactics.

The horizon was brightening with a promise of the hell to come. Slocum studied the horses. The gelding seemed somewhat recovered. The bay that bore their supplies and occasionally Joe had his head down. So did the mount Slocum had liberated from a eunuch called Abe. He had a couple of canteens and a goatskin of water. And the river was— "How far?"

"No talk!"

It was an hour, and the sun was fulfilling its promise before the wizened Indian looked back up from where he trotted pigeon-toed ahead of Slocum and the three horses. " 'Nother hour," he said.

"I mean to the river."

"How the hell I know?"

Slocum began worrying. "You don't know where we are?"

"We here. River there."

"But how far?"

"Winter, walk two day. Horse, maybe three. Summer—"

"How many days will it take us?"

"We never get there."

"We're going to die out here?" Slocum tried to get excited over the prospect, but the heat and other thoughts were getting to him.

"Horse die. We die, too, if we keep horse."

"I see."

Miles ahead, across the bare sand-gravel-soil mixture that supported tiny clumps of vegetation at one-hundred-foot intervals, he saw a plume of smoke. Now, who the hell would build a fire out here? Slocum knew he would be willing to eat his meat raw first. But Joe walked straight toward it.

Slocum began wondering why the smoke did not change shape or rise higher. It was nearly another hour before he was sure that it was not smoke at all. It was a smoke tree, which is called everything from salt cedar to tamarack and is none of these.

So Joe had been right about water. Ranchers often cursed these trees, always cut them down. They are one of nature's most efficient pumps, able to lift hundreds of gallons each day up their acres of roots, dissipating all that water uselessly into the desert air, all just to keep their pale green needles from falling off.

Was the Indian planning on tapping it the way Yankees drew sap from sugar bush?

The tree lay in a dry wash. There was not the slightest hint of dampness in the sand and gravel around it. But it *did* rain in this country—just about every time peace broke out. As they drew closer, Slocum saw other flora struggling to tap underground water. But the *chollas* and *biznagas* had not survived the last flash flood—which must have taken place during Millard Fillmore's administration.

Man and horses headed for the smoke tree's shade. Slocum waited to see what Joe would do. The Indian flopped down and went to sleep. Slocum sighed. He looked at the thirsty horses and at the goatskin. Better wait. In penance for what he was doing to the mute victims of man's schemes, he took no water himself. Slowly, the day dragged on. Slocum dozed and tried not to breathe through his drying mouth. Each time he was sure it could not turn hotter it did.

The old Indian snored steadily. The horses drooped. Finally Slocum knew neither he nor the horses could survive if he didn't tap that goatskin. He was getting to his feet when Mojave Joe awakened. "Now kill one horse."

Slocum wondered what could be wrong with a man who killed men without compunction but shuddered at the idea of doing in a horse. But the Indian was right. The horse he had taken last night was the most used up. Slocum drew his Colt and put a round through its head before he could change his mind. Joe sprang to his feet and found a pan. He slit the quivering animal's throat and caught blood, which he drank. After some initial hesitation, so did Slocum.

He wondered if it was always so salty or if this was because the animal was near death from thirst. It did little to satisfy his own, but he supposed it must be doing something. The other horses were too dispirited to spook at the smell. Joe slit the horse open and delved for liver. He found the gall bladder, slit it, and sprinkled a piece of raw liver.

"You no eat, you die. You bet."

Slocum forced himself to swallow. It was not at all

what he had expected. Rich and creamy, like some sort of cheese.

Mojave Joe grinned and thrust another piece at him. "No eat," he explained, "no teeth."

Surely this could not be the long-sought cure for scurvy. But Slocum could not recall dental problems or dentists among any Indians he had known.

"When are you going to get water?" he asked.

"No get. Too goddamn deep."

Slocum glanced at the other horses, standing with apathetic heads behind the smoke tree. "Will we get some soon? Can I give some of what we have to these poor beasts?"

"You bet. Keep 'em live two more day."

Slocum studied his Stetson and decided it was still seaworthy. He uncorked the goatskin and poured several hatfuls, alternating between the two horses. They wanted more, but he dared not pamper them. He and Joe drank sparingly, and almost immediately Slocum was overcome with a full-blown case of the scours. He wondered if it was the liver or the water or the combination. Finally his gut stopped squirming and they mounted the reviving animals. This time Joe rode, too.

Slocum had not believed it could get hotter. It did. And now Joe was angling off from the obvious trail down this broad, straight depression that ran east before them. He was forcing the horses up onto high ground, where they stumbled among head-sized boulders and shied away from bits of dead greasewood that looked like snakes. Once he had attained the ridge some fifty feet above the floor of the valley, the Indian obstinately paralleled the easier route a half mile to their left. Slocum studied the angle at which his gelding's neck drooped and wondered how much longer. He wanted to ask, but it was hot, and if he opened his mouth, he would lose another few drops of moisture. Either Mojave Joe knew what he was doing or he didn't. One thing was damned sure: Slocum didn't know.

Something strange was happening in the mountains they had left fifty miles behind. There were streaks in the afternoon sunlight, but when he glanced behind an hour later, the sky was clear again and the sun's fury undiminished.

"Water soon."

Slocum hoped so. It was hard to judge distances, but he was sure they were still less than a third of the way from mountains to river. Where were the sheriff and his rapist cronies? Slocum no longer knew whether he was ahead of or behind them. He asked Joe.

"Come soon."

Slocum gave up. Joe might know how to survive in the desert, but he was an old man, and he couldn't be that much more comfortable than Slocum was. And he regarded it as an ominous sign that the Indian was no longer walking.

He tried to remember how many men had gone with the sheriff. Nine? One man, if he lived, would not sit a horse. Slocum wondered if he had died, if his companions had put him out of his misery, or if they had abandoned him. Eight men, the sheriff—and Laura. And twenty loads of gold, plus water skins and other supplies. It must be quite a train. Probably they would travel the same way Slocum had made it so far, killing horses off as they were no longer needed.

"God damn!"

Joe's horse had rotated its ears. Slocum turned in the saddle to see what was so startling to the wrinkled Indian. The first thing he saw was that the sheriff's gold snatchers had at least fifty horses. Every one of them was galloping down the center of the trail Joe had abandoned for this rough high ground.

There were men on some horses, packs on others. They galloped loosely, exhaustedly. As he watched, one horse fell and did not rise. For an instant he thought he caught a glimpse of Laura. The sheriff was near the head of the band and making no effort to slow the stampede. Quite the contrary, the brute was lashing the ends of his reins over his mount's rump, raking it repeatedly with his spurs. Deliberately running their horses in this heat, they were heading straight toward Slocum and Joe.

Slocum dismounted, scattered Joe's bindle, and found the buffalo gun. The charge was still almost a mile away. He had to do something before they got within pistol range. He poured powder, spat an unpatched ball down the barrel, nippled a cap, and dropped prone. Squinting through the brass telescope, he aimed six feet above the spurring sheriff. Very slowly, Slocum squeezed the trigger.

"God damn!" Joe grumbled as he struggled to hold the spooked horses. "Sumbitch make big noise."

"Big holes, too," Slocum said. But it had not made one in anything he had aimed at. He poured powder and spat another ball down the barrel. This time the sheriff's horse went down. The sheriff took several seconds to get up, then caught at another man's stirrup. Still they charged on. Packhorses were scattering, and Slocum was at a loss to understand what could impel a man to be that careless of one-hundred-pound loads of treasure.

"Water come," Joe muttered.

How could he have known they would all go insane and come charging toward Slocum's buffalo gun with all their food, their gold, their water skins? Then, finally, Slocum understood what the ancient Indian was talking about.

And just as abruptly he saw why old Joe had been so anxious to get up out of that broad, low watercourse, why he had ridden instead of walked all morning as they urged the horses onward and upward. The larger party had been caught behind, where there was no high ground. Behind them, gaining rapidly, a wall of water came rolling and grumbling. It neither looked nor sounded like water. Boulders and sand flowed until the flash flood looked more like that grayish mass Slocum had occasionally seen pour from machines for mixing portland cement.

House-sized boulders growled as they struggled to grind one another to sand. And with no cloud in the sky this unheralded water came charging across the aridity in noisy witness to a thundershower fifty miles away in some mountain canyon. Flash floods. . . . The last time Slocum had seen a gullywhomper like this was on the road from Querétaro, where he had witnessed other horrors.

He loaded the buffalo gun and fired at the foremost rider. The shot was low this time, but the horse went down. Poor horses would die anyway this far from civilization. Die in minutes if they did not make the high ground ahead of that water, but Slocum couldn't surrender his hill top. He was reloading when he heard the *zup* of an arrow. Joe lay on his back, bow across his feet and pulling with both hands. Slocum got off another shot.

Abruptly it soaked into the sheriff and his companions that their dangers were not all behind them. Slocum poured powder, spat another ball into the long-barreled weapon, and squinted into the brass telescope. He swept the party for a glimpse of Laura and could not see her. He fired. He was getting the feel of the weapon now. This shot took a man in the thigh and his horse through the barrel. Both stayed down. He prayed the man would be conscious, eyes open and hurting, when the water came. Better still, he prayed the water would not kill him. Slocum wanted that for himself. He reloaded and fired.

Behind the galloping gold thieves the water was changing shape, peaking like breaking surf as the ground rose. Finally the wave collapsed, eddied, and swirled past them. Slocum was reloading when he saw his horses trotting toward the receding water. They drank hugely, swallowing appreciable quantities of sand.

Slocum wondered if the water could last long enough to refill water skin and canteens. But mostly he wondered if he could pour enough fire into these sons of a bitches to slow them down. They were so frightened of the water that they were charging right into his buffalo gun. He shifted his aim from a horse to its rider. The man's head stretched into a yard-long crimson streamer in the instant before he fell off. After that the others slowed and began looking for cover.

Slocum and Joe had it all. They crouched behind the only rocks large enough to shield a man. Slocum prayed the sheriff's men would not recognize the two strange horses that now mingled with theirs and do the obvious. There seemed little danger. They were too busy congratulating themselves on having outrun the flash flood. But soon they would settle down to the job of outgunning Slocum and Joe.

Zup! Another flint-tipped arrow whizzed. This one struck a man just above the ornate gold buckle of his gun belt. He slid off the rump of his horse. He sat in dry sand looking at the arrow that protruded from his paunch. If Slocum lived, he promised himself that either he or Joe would pull that arrow out. Preferably twisting slowly so that a loop of gut would come with it.

Where was Laura? There was no hint of anyone in woman's clothing. Then he knew what must have happened. They would have torn her clothes apart in the first frantic lunge to slake their collective lust. And later someone would know that if she was to be raped yet another day, she must be shielded from desert sun. They would have dressed her in men's clothes.

Had he shot her already?

XVIII

The packhorses tore on past Slocum's strong point. After a moment's dither the sheriff's men saw how expensive it would be to assault men who were dug in uphill with an open field of fire. They spurred away, out of range of his buffalo gun, then settled down to the job of sorting out their scattered train.

"You walk now?" Joe said.

"Reckon I'll have to." Their horses had trotted off with the others. The lot of them now milled a couple of miles east, drinking hugely from pools where the sand was settling only slightly faster than the water disappeared. "But first . . ."

Slocum went to inspect those bandits who had not ridden off. One man lay half beneath his horse and beyond all possibility of coercion. Slocum kicked dirt into sightless eyes and moved on. The next one was not Laura either. This was the one Joe had put the arrow into. Slocum was pulling it out when the old Indian said, "No."

Slocum waited.

"No pull. You break. Hard make arrow."

"All right. Let's see how you get it out."

Joe made a single slash with his knife. The arrow fell free, along with an avalanche of intestine and other organs.

"Get up and walk around a little," Slocum suggested. "Maybe you'll feel better."

The gut-shot man was straining for his pistol.

" 'Fraid not," Slocum said, and kicked it out of his reach.

"Not you. Me. Please. For God's sake!"

"Wonder if Laura said things like that. Is she still alive?"

"Yes! She's all right. God, please—"

Slocum moved on. The third victim of the buffalo gun had been drilled through the thigh. He lay with his shattered leg under a horse that still writhed and kicked. Slocum shot the horse. "What will you give me?" Slocum asked.

"For what?"

"For a quick and easy death."

"My share." The red-haired man's reply was unhesitating.

"Your share of what?"

"The gold."

"Not yours to give."

"Could I have some water?"

"How come you're not offering your share of my woman?"

"You can have that, too—" Abruptly the red-haired man realized what he was saying.

"Where is she?"

"I don't know."

"Want to die quick?"

"Yes. Oh, yes—please!"

"Try holding your breath." Slocum began walking away. He ignored the man's screamed pleas for death.

The blood on his hands had nearly all flaked off. His sleeves remained clotted and stiff. He could still hear shrill wailing as he and Joe got their kit tied into bundles and began walking east.

Slocum figured there were five left. Only five men —and Laura. Could she be aware of how he was shaving down the odds? If she was noticing anything at all, she'd have to see that the group was getting smaller. Did she know he was out there?

And he hadn't even thought about the gold. If he could just get Laura out of this, they'd have a stake. But for what?

Thanks to gang-raping Indians, she was finished back east. Now he'd have to kill every one of these animals or the word would spread around California, too. Even so, they would never be able to lead a normal life together here. He looked at his bloody sleeves. Could he ever have a normal life anywhere?

Sure. With gold he could buy a new life, even

buy a new, clean conscience. Didn't men do it all the time building churches and colleges? If he was to save Laura, he had to have at least a few loads of that gold.

First he'd have to finish the sheriff, and that wouldn't be so easy. The remaining outlaws had rounded up exhausted horses and had their pack train moving again. They were moving on freshly watered horses, with Slocum's and Joe's mounts freshly added to the remuda—moving much faster than Slocum and Joe could march with their heavy load of water.

But it was late afternoon and the flood had already passed on, leaving an altered terrain in its wake. Tomorrow a hundred kinds of flowers would bloom, shoot seed, die, and the desert would settle down to another long wait for the next gullywhomper. Slocum marched on already-tiring feet past a pool where tadpoles swam. Now, where had they been all the years since it had rained? He lay and drank of the rapidly clearing water. When he looked up, Mojave Joe was catching tadpoles ánd eating them with grinning relish.

"Le's go," the old man suggested.

Slocum began walking behind the Indian. John was nearly a foot taller, and his legs were proportionately much longer than the old man's. How was this pigeon-toed fossil managing to walk him into the ground? Old Joe was not even walking. He was trotting, bouncing along like a Chinaman with a load of laundry. Slocum studied to match his gait and couldn't. They walked another couple of miles, and he knew that no amount of raw liver or tadpoles would ever make the difference. White men just weren't meant to live in that desert.

His tongue had swollen to fill his mouth when finally the Indian slowed and spent a final mile cooling out. As they stopped in the sun's last light and stretched behind a creosote bush, the old man gave a rueful grin. "Water here," he said. "Here we hold water hole and shoot them."

The old man's plans had been aborted by a flood that changed the rules mid-game. "Do you think we can catch them now?" Slocum asked.

"You bet."

"How?" They were afoot, less than halfway across the desert, and now the sheriff and his band had more horses, fewer men to slow them down, and plenty of water.

"You wait. You see." They rested an hour. Slocum washed his feet in a puddled remnant of the torrent, did what he could for his socks, and spread them over a creosote bush. In spite of the recent flood the socks dried within minutes, and he was able to shake the sand and dust from them.

"Le's go." Resignedly, Slocum put his socks and boots back on. They started walking.

By midnight, though flowers would bloom tomorrow, every puddle had sunk into the bottomless desert's thirst. Suddenly Slocum realized he was hearing sounds not native to this place. No kit fox or kangaroo rat could make that much noise. Had to be horses. A moment later he heard voices.

He stared at Joe. The Indian did not see him, but he must have sensed Slocum's puzzlement. "Indian walk faster than horse," Joe explained in a low voice. "White man walk faster horse got bellyful sand."

Slocum remembered that gray wall of roiling water. The horses had been too thirsty to obey instinct and wait for it to settle. He wondered if they would die or if they would manage to throw if off. Damn it, his gelding and Joe's horse were among them. Dorkus had drunk that gravelly water, too! Slocum was going to walk all the way to the river.

He might as well have some fun on the way. He checked the buffalo gun. The ball he had spat into it had fallen out. He charged it with fresh powder, patched a ball, and rammed it home properly. He put a cap in the nipple and stood, swiveling his head for the sound.

Joe pointed. They began walking again. Now that he had managed a wash and clean socks, his feet didn't bother him so much, but as if to make up for this, Slocum's ankles were beginning to swell. The desert had many ways to kill a man.

But the stars were beautiful. He listened to the

desert stillness and marveled at the distances sound could travel in this clear, dry air. There was loveliness here, and at night Slocum could appreciate how the Indians had been able to live in this wasteland.

They walked at least a mile, and still he could see no hint of their prey. Joe made no special effort at concealment. It was another half mile before the Indian put finger to lips and waved Slocum to duck and make less of a silhouette in the starlight. Slocum resolved that if ever he were to cross a desert again, he would do everything possible to make that journey in the light of the moon. Where in hell were they, anyway?

Then he saw them. They were not camped. In spite of the gasping horses, the sheriff and his gang struggled to move as far as possible during the relative cool of night. Most of the horses seemed still to be there. Near the head of the train five mounts carried riders. Slocum tried to remember his body count. There ought to be another one around somewhere—unless they had got all the use they wanted out of Laura and discarded her. He and Joe stood in a tiny hollow where they would not be silhouetted and watched the pack animals go by. Then Slocum saw the extra man riding at the tail of the train. John was aiming the buffalo gun when Joe laid a warning hand on him.

Slocum wondered if he had lost count. Somebody else coming up on them? While he wondered, the opportunity for a shot disappeared. So did Mojave Joe. Slocum was turning slowly, squinting and listening, when he heard a gasp and a thump. A horse danced, then settled down to the measured *clip-clop* of the pack train.

"God damn!"

Slocum moved toward the sound of that low exclamation and found Joe grinning, his knife at the throat of a man who was so busy trying to catch his breath that he ignored the tiny cuts and trickles of blood that came with each gasp and heave.

"Your kill," Slocum said. "What will you do with him?"

"Eatum," Joe said promptly. "Eatum liver." He

removed the knife from the rider's throat long enough to slit belt and trouser front.

From the sudden and pungent odor Slocum knew the message had got through. The man was finally getting his breath back. "I didn't do nothin!" he protested.

"Nothin' of what nature?"

"I never touched her."

"But everybody else did?"

"Yeah."

Slocum turned away in disgust. "Joe, I wouldn't mind sharing a little liver with you, but don't you think we ought to cook it first."

"You bet." Joe began piling up bits of dead greasewood and *pitahaya* around the rapist. Then they were interrupted by noise from up ahead, shouts of alarm and a long cry that sounded like panic.

"What else did you do?" Slocum asked.

"Cut throat fifteen packhorse."

"Slocum!"

Slocum remembered that voice from San Bernardino. He had no intention of giving away his position.

"Over here!" It was the candidate for liver-roasting, his voice shrill with desperation.

"Don't kill him!" Slocum warned.

There was an abrupt, rabbitlike shriek and a jetting fountain of blood. "Now what in hell'd you have to go do?" Slocum growled as they moved silently away from the wailing, shrieking rapist.

"Cut off cock," Joe explained. "Leave handle. Hang on, he live. Maybe live long time."

After Professor Moriarty had despaired of forcing mathematics into Slocum, there had been a spell when it had been thought the boy might be a doctor. Like any healthy boy, Slocum had pored over his *Gray's Anatomy* long enough to memorize the interesting parts. He remembered the huge blood vessels of the *bulbus cavernosus*. The man could die in minutes. Or he could squeeze for dear life—if life was still dear.

"Slocum!"

They waited while the sheriff and two others moved

with elaborate caution toward the shrieker who held his life in his hand.

"Slocum, I got something belongs to you!"

Why do you think I'm following you? But Slocum did not voice his thoughts. The best he could do for Laura was not to advertise his presence. Why had he let hubris come between himself and his girl? Was vengeance more important than her safety? It must have been, in that moment of madness when he had lectured his first victim on the value of advertising.

Why couldn't he have kept his damn-fool mouth shut? So they would have known somebody was following, killing them. Did they have to know that Laura was the lever by which he could be moved?

To hell with this cat-and-mouse game. He patted his Colts and began moving back toward the one who still held the remains of his life in bloody hands.

But the sheriff and his apostles were not walking into that trap. They were circling the keening mourner of a lost phallus, hunting his hunter. Slocum could hear them, but he could not see them. Damn these moonless nights! The desert stars were brilliant beyond all belief, but they were no substitute for a moon. There was a cloying, honeysuckle sweetness around him. My God, were the flowers blooming already?

Then abruptly he smelled tobacco, the rank goat stink of unwashed mankind. Slocum froze. He extended his hand palm down and fingers spread. He rotated it until he felt a faint coolness between his fingers. He turned cautiously until he was facing that way, then looked slightly to one side.

Less than ten feet away a man stared blindly toward him. Slocum drew a Colt and took careful aim. Then he agonized for several seconds while his target stood frozen as a jacklighted deer. This man merited more than a quick bullet. Slocum wanted to disable him and return later to pay another installment on Laura's account. But there were two others out here somewhere. Survival was more important. He squeezed the trigger, and in the flash from the Colt's barrel he saw the man's head abruptly change shape.

One down, two to go. The rest of the party, he supposed, were up there trying to get the train back together, to reshuffle packs now that they had fifteen fewer horses. Where was Mojave Joe? Where were the sheriff and that other son of a bitch who were gunning for him?

Or had he got the sheriff? He didn't think so. The man he had shot was too thin. Even in starlight that gross horse killer would be easy to pick out. A yard-long flame streaked from a rifle, and Slocum felt the ball part air over his head.

He resisted the temptation to move. Instead, he lay inert as a rock with the Colt aimed where the rifle had fired. His heart pumped a hundred thirty beats before curiosity got the better of somebody who stood to see what he had hit. Slocum shouldered him. As the man spun, Slocum put another ball into his midsection. He lay smiling quietly in the darkness, knowing neither would be immediately fatal.

Somebody had had enough. He was charging off, running bent over, more intent on distance than concealment. "That you, Sheriff?" Slocum called. "If 'tis, you might remember that if the girl's gone, then you've lost your last chip."

There was no reply. Slocum moved toward the man he had shot. He wasn't sure, but he thought this one had been called Bryant. The man lay gasping. Slocum surveyed his wounds. He would surely die from the one in his belly, even if the shoulder wound were not to fester. "Think you'll live to see the light of day?" Slocum asked.

The man with two holes in him was too busy trying to breathe.

"How was she?" Slocum asked. "Nice-looking woman and all that, but do you really think she was worth this?"

Still no reply.

"You'll live till tomorrow," Slocum said comfortingly. "You'll see daylight again." To make sure of it, he cut off the groaning man's eyelids before he moved back to look for his Indian partner.

"God damn!" Joe said in greeting.

"I'm afraid I probably am. And what have you been up to?"

"Kill more horse. They got hell of a time carry gold now."

Slocum smiled. He was sure the sheriff was still alive. Laura, too—unless they were bluffing. Which made two more men besides the beefy Bigelow. The odds were getting better all the time. "How far to the river?"

" 'Bout halfway."

"Think we'll make it all right?"

"No."

XIX

"Why not? We've got water."

"You don' walk good 'nough."

"If you feel that way, why didn't you steal a couple of horses instead of killing them all?"

"Horses dying. Too much sand."

"All of them?"

"Not all. Some don't drink mud."

"Sounds to me like they're still trying to sort things out up there. Why don't we slip in and borrow a couple of good horses before they can move out again."

"No."

"Why not?"

"Wind come."

"I could use a little."

"You won' like."

Fifteen minutes later Slocum understood. The wind was not particularly strong, less than forty miles an hour, but it picked up every jagged grain of sand and fine gravel for its one-hundred-mile fetch. It threw sand at them until Slocum was certain the wind hated him personally. Every grain seemed aimed directly at him, and even through his shirt it stung. He glanced down unbelievingly at his Colts. The polished brown wood of the grips was now rough and white. The blueing had been sandblasted from barrels and cylinders until the pistols were gray. His belt, his boots, his holsters, were losing their polish and turning to suede.

He wondered how the man without eyelids was making out. Slocum would have been skinned raw and bleeding long ago if he had not wrapped an extra shirt around his head and shoulders.

They lay the rest of the night and several hours

into the morning before the wind died down. Finally Joe jerked at Slocum's ankle, and John stood erect.

It was amazing. Down near the ground, the wind-blown sand was bad as ever, but now that the wind was dying, it only blew waist high. They looked out over an undulating carpet of sand that made their feet invisible. It was like wading.

Slocum looked for the pack train. No sign. Then he began to recognize the hummocks where sand had drifted around dead horses. As if the poor beasts hadn't had enough in their stomachs already!

"You want gold?" Joe asked.

Slocum laughed. Each of those hummocks of sand held one hundred pounds of gold. What good was it? Trade it all for a drink of clean water and a way out of here. Then he realized one of those poor beasts just might have died carrying a water skin.

Without a shovel it was slow work. It took him a while to realize what must have happened to the rest of the train. The sheriff, his few remaining followers, and possibly Laura would have wrapped their faces and those of their mounts against the sand. On horseback they could have moved out at least an hour ahead of a man on foot, which meant they had saved a few horses and their gold.

"Can you find this place again?" Slocum asked. "A lot of men died for this gold. It shouldn't be lost again."

"I find. Men on mountains watch us. They find, too."

"What men?"

"Not know. Saw light flash from mountains. Nobody come down, but somebody watch, you bet."

Slocum looked southward toward the towering San Bernardino Mountains. It was hard to estimate distances, but the mountains must be a good fifteen miles away, maybe farther. Who was watching them? Had the citizen posse come back looking for the sheriff and his loot? In this clear desert air good eyes with field glasses would see a lot of details. Slocum laughed softly to himself. The gold wouldn't be lost again—not that it mattered. There was nobody close enough to help, even if he wanted help.

And do I want help? he asked himself. No. I think not. It's too late for that. Too late for anything. But by Jesus I can make Sheriff Bigelow pay!

In the end it was Joe who found water. They poured it carefully from skin to skin and managed to get something with less solid content than the hastily gathered mud of their own supply. By now the wind had died to an occasional sandy gust that felt as if it came from a Bessemer furnace. Slocum pulled the cylinders from his Colts and began picking sand from the mechanism.

The Colts were so jammed he could not cock them. He studied the bore. The guns no longer had any blue on their outer surfaces, but the inside of the barrels seemed unaffected. He guessed they would still shoot once he had held them upside down and tapped long enough to dislodge the last grain of sand from totally dry locks. Would the oily fat from a dead horse lubricate them? Nothing he smeared on them could smell worse than Slocum did now. *My kingdom for a bath.* But he didn't have a kingdom. Nor a queen. . . .

"Le's go," Joe said.

Slocum got to his feet. As he walked, he continued tapping sand from the pistols. Soon he would need them again. Lurking in the corners of his mind was the knowledge that he might be forced to . . . The sheriff was running scared. What might he try next with Laura? Would Slocum be forced to kill her, too? Before this was over, a quick death might be the best he could do for her. Jesus! First Indians and now white men. Some girls had all the luck.

He asked himself if it could have turned out any other way. If he'd used a little more restraint? Acted "civilized"? What difference would it have made? They had raped her repeatedly long before they suspected he had survived the housewarming prepared for him, for Cavanaugh, and for her poor demented father. Retraint and civilization had no place with scum like this.

But you lower yourself to their level, his demon insisted.

Or elevate myself. He remembered the shock in Mojave Joe's wrinkled face after that first act of vengeance. He wondered if any of these blackguards—if he were to let them get to a courtroom, could a smart lawyer get them off? It had happened before. Slocum could remember once, a long time ago, being taught to respect the law. But that was before the Yankee occupation of the South.

It hardly mattered. None of them would outlive him. At worst he could see to that.

"God damn!"

"I beg your pardon?"

Joe pointed. They had left the watercourse now and were crossing an endless beachlike plain of tiny windrows punctuated by occasional clumps of vegetation. Heat and dust devils obscured the horizon, but above the shimmery line that divided heaven from earth a caravan walked in stately progress across the sky. Slocum squinted as the image shimmered, dissolved, then reappeared upside down and ten degrees higher. Riders were bunched at the head of the train, and one brought up the rear behind a dozen strung-out pack animals. As they watched, one horse fell *up* and lay motionless on the inverted desert floor.

Slocum lay on his back and aimed the buffalo gun at the mirage. He didn't know whether the telescope would be effective, but it did magnify the image. That slightly built rider in the middle who rode in head-down apathy—that had to be Laura. She was alive. "How far away are they?" he asked.

Mojave Joe knew no more than Slocum did of refraction or of how far mirages carried over the horizon. But both knew how many hours it had been since they had been near the train. Those moribund horses couldn't be more than five or ten miles ahead.

The man at the rear cut the dead horse loose and urged the remaining beasts on, making no effort to salvage the dying animal's pack. Slocum wished he'd spent more time shooting horses. Might have been over by now if he had been less keen on making those sons of bitches pay for what they had done. . . . But probably not. One reason two men had brought down twenty was the terror the twenty had felt.

The train got moving again, heads down and stumbling. The rear guard mounted his horse and it collapsed. He was running after the pack train and waving his arms when the image shimmered and disappeared.

"God damn!" Joe marveled.

"You know what causes that?" Slocum asked.

"You say?"

Slocum pointed to the sky. "Why?"

The Indian seemed embarrassed.

"No sin to be ignorant," Slocum said. "I don't know, either."

It took Joe, in his limited English, a moment to digest the meaning; then he began to mumble. Slocum heard "Ometecutli" and recalled that this god was responsible for fault zones and earthquakes.

It was an hour and a half before they came upon the man whose horse had died. Though he wore a single Colt, he was unable to draw it. "What's wrong with you ignorant bastards?" Slocum asked. "We're carrying enough water, and we don't have horses."

The man was so far gone he could only move his mouth and make croaking noises. Joe produced his knife. But Slocum said, "No."

They gave him water, and hope grew in the dying man's eyes. After a few minutes and another drink he was able to explain. "Plenty of water. Had enough to get across with one third of the horses even without that flash flood."

Slocum began to suspect which way this conversation would go. He waited.

"That bitch of a girl. Don't know how she did it, but the plug came out of every skin and canteen. Ain't been a drop of piss between us for half a day."

Slocum smiled. Laura was still alive, still thinking. She knew horses and—Jesus, did she ever know men by now! He had to catch up soon. With certain death facing them, what could the sheriff and his remaining deputy lose? Maybe they had killed her already. He directed his smile to the man who had given him this information. "I'm truly glad you drank that water," he explained. "Now you'll take at least twelve more hours to die. Anything I would do would only hasten the end. I trust you'll learn to pray and have time to meditate on the unforgiving nature of any god who would create this kind of country. Come to think of it, I can do you another favor." He pried open the rapist's eyes and filled them with sand.

Slocum tipped his hat, and they walked off with their water bags, plus this man's knife and pistol. Joe threw the knife away as soon as they were out of sight. He studied the high-hammered Peacemaker doubtfully and finally stuffed it into the waistband of his rugged jeans.

"You soft," Joe commented. "Why you don't take hat, shirt?"

"Because if I leave them, he lives a couple of hours longer."

"Crazy sumbitch! This good place. Why you think gods bad?"

Slocum was startled. He had not expected Joe to catch that.

"Lots badder places. You ever see big bad water? Rain all time. Cold. Head hurt."

Slocum had never thought of the seacoast that way. "Every man sees heaven a different way," he conceded. "My own would be a place where everyone spoke English instead of that accursed Yankee twang."

"They die now," Joe said.

"Chances are they don't see this desert as heaven, either. Don't you ever wish it could be a trifle less hot?"

"Damn cold winter." Joe seemed suddenly embarrassed.

"What is it?"

"They die. They want die happy."

Slocum sighed. He knew what the old Indian was trying to tell him. By now the poor girl would have been raped so many times that once more—but dying men might choose to act out more deadly fantasies.

"Le's go." He said it even though they were already going as fast as Slocum could walk in rapidly disintegrating boots.

They walked right through the hottest part of the day, and late that afternoon the train was visible. For an hour those horses that still lived struggled on. Then finally nothing moved. Slocum wondered if the sheriff and his single remaining apostle were dead or dying. Would they kill Laura first? He glanced at Joe.

The Indian shrugged. "Horse got water inside."

Slocum wondered if the sheriff would think of that. Probably. He'd chosen to come to the desert. It would be best to close cautiously. They crept forward.

Nothing happened.

Heart sinking, Slocum moved closer. If the men were dead, there was little hope that Laura would be alive. There were only four horses, standing head-down and ready to drop. The rest had dropped long ago. There was a terrible temptation to rush blindly ahead with drawn guns. He managed to resist it, reminding himself that these two men were the survivors and therefore the toughest. Facing death, they had nothing to lose. They would spend their final hours dissecting Slocum with the same satanic joy that had suffused him. And Laura?

Joe moved away and circled cautiously to approach from the opposite side. The sun was near setting but the heat still near unbearable. And if Laura had dumped their water, there would be no way she could have saved any small store for herself. Slocum crept closer.

As he approached the camp, Slocum abruptly saw that the sheriff wasn't as bad off as he had thought. These horses were tired but not that close to death. Somebody had been rationing water to these four. He came still closer and discovered that the men were not that near death, either.

Slocum wondered if he had gone mad. The heat, the thirst, the terrible revenge he had taken on those other men—how many times had he watched Laura being raped? Was he seeing it now, or imagining it? The sheriff was nowhere in sight, but Laura was—

naked, spread-eagled atop a horse blanket. He squinted through the brass telescope and saw that she had been staked out Indian fashion. Her body was bruised and scratched.

But she was alive. If he could get her away from here, someplace where she could forget—

She would never forget. No one forgets things like this. But with patience, with tenderness and love, perhaps she could again realize that all men were not evil. He'd helped her once. . . .

And now he was aiming a buffalo gun at her, and holding it with bloodstained hands.

She seemed more dead than alive, hardly moving except to breathe. She would have learned long ago how impossible it is for a human limb extended full length to pull up a stake. But if she lay there in the sun much longer, no matter how quietly, she'd die.

Slocum could see only one man. Not the sheriff. The man was lashing packs and redistributing gear among their few remaining horses. He took his time with the lashing, but then, finally, turned to the naked girl. He went to kneel at her head. He leaned over her, grasping a breast in each hand, kneading them as he—

Slocum gasped, and red rage filmed his vision. The son of a bitch was stuffing his cock down the helpless girl's throat. Her chest heaved as she gagged and struggled to breathe. Slocum wiped his eyes, then coldly and carefully checked the cap on the buffalo gun. He took in a deep breath, let out half, and was still working at holding the dancing cross hairs still when something struck him from behind.

Slocum woke to pain. He was staring straight up into the sun. Then suddenly he was in shadow. His eyes wouldn't focus on the image above him, but the voice was unmistakable.

"Fine figure of a woman," the sheriff said conversationally. "Liked her the first time I saw her. Told myself you was a lucky man. But I reckon everybody's luck has to play out sooner or later."

There wasn't much to say to that.

"So now I got the girl and the gold," the sheriff said. "Girl won't last a lot longer, but the gold will."

"The Pinkertons will trail you forever," Slocum said.

"Reckon they'll try," the sheriff said. He kept his voice low, almost friendly. "But, you see, I been planning this for a long time."

"Bullshit. You didn't know about the gold," Slocum said.

"Nope. But I been planning on lighting out. Not everything that gets blamed on Vásquez was his doing. I had me a nice little pile stashed away. Another year or so and I'd take it and split. Then Cavanaugh came along and my pile didn't seem so big. Looked like a good time to leave San Bernardino."

The big man moved away, and once more the sun was in Slocum's eyes. He tried to move and found that he'd been staked out like Laura, wrists and ankles stapled to the ground with forked pieces of some thorny desert shrub. He rolled his head and found that he was almost within reach of Laura's naked body. She was still gasping and sobbing, but the other man was not there.

"Laura—"

She didn't answer.

"You've used some of my people kind of poorly," Sheriff Bigelow said. "Some of them was family. You shouldn't have done that. 'Course, you did do me a kind of favor by makin' for fewer ways to share, so I reckon I owe you something."

"That's real kind of you," Slocum managed.

Bigelow laughed. "Yep. So I ain't going to cut your balls off. Fact is, I ain't going to do a thing to you." He turned and called, "Fergus, we 'bout ready to head out?"

There was no answer.

The sheriff sighed. "Guess it's taking him a while to find your horse. So as long as there's nothing else to do, I might as well get in a last one. Sort of for old time's sake. Best look at how well you're fastened first, though." He came over and examined the stakes holding Slocum down. "Right fine," he reported.

He unbuckled his belt and leaned over Laura, exactly as had the man Slocum had been aiming at. John struggled, but the stakes held. There was no leverage at all.

"You watch real good," the sheriff said. He stuffed his cock into Laura's mouth, then bent to fondle and knead her breasts. "You watchin' now?" he asked.

After a few minutes the sheriff ignored Slocum. He was too caught up in his own amusement. He leaned further, nuzzled and bit her belly while Laura gasped and gagged and moaned.

Later Slocum would be able to analyze his emotions and know that the scene, horror unbounded, was doubly devastating to him because he loved this girl, desired her with all his heart. And even as he watched the sheriff pumping at her head, the real horror was that Slocum found it arousing. He had never known that such things lay buried deep inside him. He prayed that he would live long enough to kill the bastard who had forced this bitter self-knowledge upon him.

The sheriff was approaching his climax, nearly crushing the girl's head with the plunging of his huge body. His legs spread until one was actually touching Slocum's hand. Suddenly Slocum knew there might be a God after all. He was staked out by the wrists and ankles, but if he could just get a solid grip on something that would pull his hand upward. . . .

He grasped the sheriff's ankle and hung on to his only chance. Then he filled his lungs.

"Laura! *Now!*" he shouted.

She was alive. She was conscious. She heard him. From the depths of her misery she found the strength for one final effort.

Sheriff Bigelow howled and thrashed as her teeth closed around his cock at the first spurt of his release. His leg kicked involuntarily. Slocum hung on and pulled with all his strength.

The sheriff was still howling and thrashing, kicking in agony and pounding Laura's ears, when Slocum shook the stake free from his hand and reached over to free his other. He was getting his legs freed when the sheriff looked up, startled. The big man's fist crashed into Laura's throat, and Bigelow pulled free.

The sheriff's pistol was entangled in his pants. Bigelow scrabbled for the weapon, but Slocum's pointed boot caught him under the chin. The sheriff sprawled backward, and Slocum leaped onto him, driving his knees into Bigelow's stomach. Then he sat on the sheriff's chest and pounded at his face, striking him again and again, hitting him long after the sheriff had gone out.

He was still pounding at the sheriff's head when Laura screamed again. "John!"

Her eyes were wide with horror. Slocum turned to see where she was looking. The other man was coming back. He saw Slocum and drew.

Slocum rolled behind the sheriff. Now it was Slocum's turn to try to untangle the sheriff's Colt from the trousers around Bigelow's ankles. The outlaw ran forward, and Slocum knew he would be too late. The other man was too close, and the pistol was still entangled.

The man pitched forward onto his face. An arrow stuck out of his back.

Slocum could breathe again. "Joe?"

"Who you think?" Mojave Joe stood directly behind the fallen outlaw. "God damn, that good shot," he said. "Not sure I hit him, that far away. Good shot."

"You bet," Slocum said. Then he tried to stand, and fell.

He was out only for a moment. When he recovered, Mojave Joe was pouring water into his mouth. Slocum coughed and swallowed. "I'm okay," he said. "If I was that bad off from just a few minutes—" He took the canteen and went to free Laura.

She screamed when she saw him, but then her eyes focused. "John—"

He pulled the stakes away, then sat beside her and cradled her against him, holding the canteen. She drank greedily. Then once more her eyes were filled with horror. She looked at Mojave Joe and screamed.

"No, no. He's our friend," Slocum said.

Laura screamed once more and fainted.

They covered Laura's nakedness and rigged a blanket to give her shade; then Slocum used half a canteen of water to wash her. She hadn't drunk enough, and the evaporating water might cool her. Her skin felt dry and warm.

She was alive, and the ordeal was over. Did she know that? She lay gasping, totally unconscious. Slocum washed her again. There didn't seem to be anything else he could do.

"Now for those two," he said.

"Eatum liver?" Joe asked.

"All right with me."

"Get arrow first. That good arrow. You bet."

The sheriff's companion was unconscious, and from the blood that poured out after Joe liberated his arrow Slocum didn't think the man would ever wake. He cursed lightly under his breath and went to examine the sheriff.

Bigelow lay on his back. He breathed noisily through a smashed nose and puffed lips that concealed missing teeth. Slocum thoughtfully rolled him on his side so he wouldn't drown in his own blood. An ant had already discovered the trickle of blood from Bigelow's cock.

Slocum looked at him in disgust. This was the man who'd started it all. If any of the sheriff's band had deserved the horrors Slocum had been dealing out, Bigelow did. But now that it was over, Slocum knew he'd never be able to torture the sheriff. Not in cold blood, not like that. Better simply to shoot him.

But not until he woke up and knew it was coming. He deserved that much, anyway. Slocum found a length of rope, cut it in three, and tied Bigelow's wrists and ankles, then bowed him backward so that his hands and feet were together and tied that way. Then he used a cup of water to douse the sheriff's head.

The sheriff woke moaning. He tried to look up at Slocum, but he couldn't focus. One eye was swollen closed to a pinpoint. The other was wide.

He tried to say something, but John couldn't understand him.

At the sound of Bigelow's voice, Laura began screaming again. Slocum went to her and knelt beside her. "It's me. John. It's all right; it's over. We can go home now."

She screamed again.

He put his arms out to hold her, and she shrank away. "Don't touch me!" She collapsed into sobbing hysteria.

"It's me, Laura. John. I won't hurt you."

She wouldn't look at him.

"You've got to drink some water," Slocum said. "If you don't, you'll collapse."

She screamed again. Her face was flushed and her skin fiery red. Slocum knew she'd have to drink soon or she'd die. He took her arm. She shrank away, screaming again and again. Finally he left the canteen beside her. When he was out of her sight, she opened it and drank avidly, but her eyes stared wildly, and she looked around, never lifting her head to look more than a few feet away. As long as no one was near, she did not scream, but when Slocum tried to go to her, she turned away and shrieked.

There were a dozen ants on the sheriff's cock now. Slocum reached instinctively to brush them away. Then he looked back at Laura, and put his hand in his pocket.

XX

They moved on at sundown. By then the sheriff's midsection was alive with the ants. Slocum didn't bother to find out if Bigelow was still alive. He certainly wouldn't be in the morning.

The last of the rapists was finished. The gold was scattered across forty miles of the Mojave. With sundown Laura was no longer in danger of heat stroke, but she would not let John come close to her. When he tried, she screamed, a voiceless, wordless sound of terror that tore at John's guts.

"We have about one day's water," Slocum said. "Which way?"

Joe pointed southwest. "Maybe we get to mountain. Water in mountain."

"Will the horses get there?" Slocum asked.

Joe shrugged. "We get there. Maybe one horse get there. More don't know."

They got Laura aboard a horse. She still screamed and stood in the stirrups to ease her abused crotch, but instinct kept her in the saddle.

Slocum hefted the sheriff's saddlebags. They were heavy with gold. After a moment's thought, Slocum dropped the bags to the ground and mounted the sheriff's outsize horse. Laura couldn't walk. One horse had to survive until they reached water. Carrying gold wouldn't help the odds.

They had gone two miles when they came upon the first dead horse. There was gold in its pack. "Think you could find these next winter if we came out with water and a few mules?"

"You bet," Joe said. " 'Less wind come."

A sandstorm could bury the treasure for another hundred years. But, strung out as the horses were, no storm would bury them all. If he and the Indian could just come back in the cool months, they could recover enough treasure to last a lifetime. And what could he do about Laura? Was there the slightest hope she would ever recover from the madness that had descended upon her?

Near midnight they passed another dead horse with its hundred pounds of gold. Slocum was still fresh, but the horses were drooping. Joe had long since slipped from his mount and trotted pigeon-toed at the head of the column. Laura's screams had degenerated into a constant wheezing sob. He wanted to give her water, but each time he came near, she threw up her hands and renewed her shrieking. After she tried once to spur her horse over Joe, who jogged ahead, he took the reins and led her. And still she stood in the stirrups.

What was he going to do? As he listened to her screams, Slocum saw how shallow was his commitment. In sickness and in health, for better or for worse, forsaking all others— It had been a wonderful dream. But as he studied this remainder of a woman, Slocum knew that he was not made of such stern stuff, that even if she had come unscathed from this ordeal, soon he would tire of an honest life. He would tire even sooner of an honest woman. Could he have done anything differently? Perhaps. But he had not. And he could not change the past.

"Think we'll find water?" he asked.

"You bet."

It was encouraging to know that Joe was cheerful. Without consultation they stopped and made camp. Joe sneaked up on Laura from behind and pinioned her arms while Slocum poured water into her. After a moment she stopped struggling and swallowed willingly enough.

"Don't you know me?" he asked. "It's Slocum. You'll be all right now." He put a hand toward her, and even in the starlight he could see the whites as her eyes widened. Joe shook his head and stayed behind. As long as the Indian remained out of sight, she seemed less distraught.

They tried to sleep, and he woke with a start just in

time to escape the boulder that Laura struggled to bring down on his head. After that they tied her and took turns sitting guard. There was little left of the grin on Joe's wrinkled face by the time light appeared and they resumed their march toward the mountains.

It was mid-morning when their water gave out, and midday before Joe called a halt in a dry wash that looked as arid as the rest of the desert. He began digging with a pointed stick and a tin plate. A yard down, the sand no longer crumbled. Another foot, and mud seeped into the hole. It was midafternoon before they had filled water skins and canteens and resumed their journey.

Slocum tried to remember where he was. They passed an occasional dead horse, so he must have passed through this way, but it all looked alike, equally deadly and dry, and Jesus, he would give what was left of his soul for a bath!

"God damn!"

Slocum looked up. Outlined in the low afternoon sun was a smudge of something not native to the desert. He squinted and could not make it out. An hour later, in the sun's last glimmer, he aimed the buffalo gun and squinted through the telescope. Several miles ahead across the barren flat, a proper column of armed men with well-fed horses and a baggage train of wagons were moving toward them. At the head of the column a man in officer's kepi was looking toward Slocum through field glasses. Hastily, Slocum lowered the buffalo gun. The last damned thing he needed was another fight.

In the hour before darkness they watched outriders spread until it would be impossible to outflank the approaching column. Laura was still screaming, still standing in the stirrups, and they had been forced to lash her hands to the saddle horn. Slocum glanced at Joe. "No use of you getting caught," he said.

"You bet!" The Indian resurrected his grin for an instant, then slipped from his horse and disappeared. Slocum knew the old man would have no trouble slipping through the outriders. As for himself, even without the problem of Laura he didn't care. He was at loose ends and tired of life. Tired especially of the terms on which he had been forced to live it. Would there be no end to killing?

The column approached, and suddenly Slocum saw they were not wagons at all. They were high, solid-wheeled ox carts. *Carretas,* they had called them down south. Now he recognized the shape of that officer's kepi. Ought to. He'd shot at enough of them while serving the emperor. Was this the same lot who had tried to take the gold up where he had first dug it from the Jesuits' hiding place? How had the *juaristas* got wind of it? Must have known of it, but not where.

Now the Frenchman's miraculous "escape" made sense. The legionnaires had been followed.

He continued riding toward the head of the column, leading Laura's horse. She saw the dark faces and uniforms of a hundred riders, and she found new voice for her screams. The man at the head of the column wore the triple silver bars of a *capitán primero.* His face was stony. "Release her immediately."

Slocum raised his hands. "My wife has suffered enough. Will you do still more to her?"

The captain's face was unbelieving. He untied Laura and received parallel red furrows down his face for the trouble. It took two *pelones* to hold her while a sergeant managed to tie her again. "You were saying?" Slocum addressed the captain.

"Your wife?" the captain asked. "Following a trail of gold and mutilation across the desert, it looked more like a falling-out of thieves."

"The thieves stole my wife and tried to kill me. Surely you'll not fault me for trying to save my woman."

"But such vengeance—"

"La venganza es un invento humano," Slocum snapped. "And I'll give you one guess whose country taught me that proverb."

"But you were there when the gold was dug up."

"Of course I was. I led them to it."

The captain was unable to conceal his astonishment. Briefly, Slocum told him of the Carlist offer to Jefferson Davis, how the Yankees had tormented Laura's father for the secret, of Cavanaugh's misplaced trust in the local law and what the sheriff and his men had done to Cavanaugh, to Slocum, to General van Arnem and to his daughter. . . .

"Ahora comprendo," the captain said. "But you must admit it would seem to an outsider that you were all in it together and merely squabbling over how to divide." He paused and struggled to put a point to his drooping mustache. "And now that you've killed them all, what of the gold?"

"Gold's nice to have. But note that as I make my way out of this garden of God, I bring only a woman who's no longer of any earthly use to anyone. Should you find gold among my effects, melt it and I'll drink it."

"Then you have no objection if we recover it for the cause?"

"¿Cual causa?"

"La causa juarista."

"Oh, my God!" Slocum shook his head. "Are you an innocent, or a scoundrel?"

The captain's face turned several shades darker. "One need not ask on what side you fought. Have you never considered that of the infinite number of ways to do evil, the one truly unforgivable sin is to enlist in a foreign cause and fight for something which does not concern you? If the French and Americans and all the others would fight their wars on their own territory, I'm sure we would settle our differences adequately with our own fallings-out."

Slocum shrugged. "But your hero was a Yankee puppet. Didn't your newspapers tell of his offers to sell Baja California, sell a right-of-way from El Paso to Mazatlán, which in due time would have made everything north of that line Yankee? What of his huckstering of the Isthmus of Tehuantepec for an ocean-to-ocean roadway—order to be preserved with U.S. troops?"

It was the Mexican's turn to shrug. "Fortunately you *gringos* were too busy with your own fallings-out to accept any of those offers. In any event, if your

Davis would bargain with *carlistas* . . . A patriot does not what he *would* but what he *must*. A piece of country in Mexican hands seemed preferable to all of it under some Austrian adventurer with an imperfect knowledge of Spanish—and so little confidence in himself that he would not renounce his claims to European thrones. Intruders can always go elsewhere if their adventure fails. Where do we go after you're finished ruining our country?"

"It was in fair shape while Kaiser Max lived."

"And in better shape under Juárez. While Don Benito lived, the people loved him."

"And now he's dead and you're without a leader —same sort of adventurer as I."

"I work for *my* country. Also *in* what was, until recently, my country."

Slocum sighed. His home country was occupied, too.

"Since Juárez died, a rascal named Díaz weeps over his tomb, effacing memory of the mischief he caused while Don Benito lived. If freedom is to survive, we must have money and arms."

Slocum shrugged. He had fought that Yankee puppet of a Juárez, who had fought the emperor, who had usurped— "Who cares? Obviously you're going to take it anyway."

"Those . . . things we keep finding—did you kill them all?"

Slocum glanced at Laura, who still screamed. She had been raped by Indians and whites. Now she awaited the same from Mexicans. "My sole regret is that I could not have done it more slowly and painfully."

The captain seemed torn between horror and amusement. "You were of the emperor's legion."

"While the emperor lived, there was stability and order."

"There is order in graveyards. Will you join us?"

Slocum stared.

"You're a brave man and able," the captain said.

Slocum shook his head. "Considering the utter rascality of your opponents, yours may be the better choice at the moment. But do you know what you're asking?"

The captain did not.

"I've picked the losing side in two wars. Three, if you include this affair. Will you scuttle your last hope by enlisting a Jonah?"

The captain laughed. "What will you do?" he finally asked.

Slocum shrugged and glanced at Laura, who cringed from these soldiers. *"¡Déjenla en paz!"* he snarled. They obeyed the voice of authority and left her alone. Still she screamed.

The captain raised his eyes to the sky, but there was no answer there. "How much more gold lies ahead of us?" he asked.

"All the rest of it. Three or four loads."

"Will you help us find it?"

"It beats walking home without water."

The captain gave orders, and Laura was passed into one of the ox-drawn supply *carretas* where *soldaderas* did what they could for her. Surrounded by women, and no longer astride a horse, she became manageable. But later that night, when Slocum looked in on her, she still screamed at the sight of a man.

Morning came, and they had recovered the rest of the gold. Outriders had found several of Slocum's victims, among them the sheriff. Coyotes and foxes had been at them until it was difficult to know where Slocum had left off. He volunteered no information, and the captain refrained from asking unnecessary questions. Everyone was feeling the strain of that incessant screaming.

"How many days back to San Bernardino?" Slocum asked.

The captain gave a ghost of a smile. "You think we would enter a town and start another war? We've enemies enough now."

Slocum had not thought of this.

"You wish to return to San Bernardino?" the captain said.

Slocum had no reason to go back. He could not recall a single nice thing happening to him in that miserable hotbed of factionalism. "All I really want to do is figure out what to do about her."

The captain's air was tentative. "If she would, she might beg for release."

"I've killed enough men. I'll not kill women." Slocum turned to face the captain. "Nor am I closing my eyes while somebody else puts my wife out of her misery."

"Tienes razón," the captain agreed. "We must all draw the line somewhere. But what will you do?"

Slocum didn't know. "Where will you go?" he asked the captain.

"South."

The border, Slocum thought, lay about one hundred miles south—slightly farther away than the river. But there had to be water holes somewhere along the way. Down near where he had first entered California, at the Yuma crossing, there was a miniature Coulter's Hell of geysers and boiling mud pots. He recalled that some optimist had hoped to attract gawkers, as they were starting to do up on the Yellowstone.

He rode beside the captain at the head of the column, wishing he could join the men out at the point—wishing he could be anywhere out of range of the screams that came periodically from that *carreta.*

Suddenly it looked as if his wish would be granted. Up ahead, at the point, some *pelón* was shooting. As he looked at the captain, it turned into a fusillade.

"Looks like somebody else wants that gold," Slocum said. The captain was too busy deploying his men to reply.

XXI

By the time the attackers were ready to throw their full weight, the captain had his *pelones* dug in and readied. Slocum watched with some amusement as the townspeople of San Bernardino discovered the difference between truth and propaganda—which is roughly the difference between seasoned troops and unprepared rabble victimized by their belief in destiny.

"It was not this easy when you fought against me," the captain observed as he made another effort to twist a point into his heat-sodden mustache. "Those men are too stupid to merit the title 'fool.' "

Slocum shrugged. "Don't be too sure. Out there you have the solid citizens. Grocery clerks to the last man. But somewhere along your flank you may have the newly respectable legions of Captains Crowley and Giraud."

The captain raised his eyebrows.

"Those who first dug up the gold," Slocum said. "Alliances must have changed rather swiftly once the townspeople learned the way their sheriff was going."

"And where do you stand?"

"I stand for Slocum."

"And for Mrs. Slocum," the captain guessed.

Slocum nodded. He began going over his sand-blasted Colts. The posse had not lost all that many men, but, being inexperienced, they had abruptly discovered what everybody knows but only old soldiers believe—that bullets can actually kill and that death is deplorably permanent. Their charge had failed, as cavalry charges will always fail against prepared infantry, and now the grocery clerks were out of range, licking their wounds, blaming one another—totally unable to understand how all this carnage could have come from a bunch of goddamn Mexicans. It was in direct violation of all the laws of God and man.

They would already be calculating the waterless miles back to San Bernardino, wondering whatever had got into them to come this far on a wild goose chase over some goddamn gold that probably didn't even exist, and where in hell were all those old Southerners and crazy Frenchmen who were supposed to be helping out?

Slocum studied the terrain with some curiosity. That ill-advised charge had found even rougher going when the horses had slowed and nearly fallen going through a twenty-foot strip of soft ground that seemed freshly plowed. The strip ran in a nearly straight line, disappearing in both directions. In grassland it might have been a firebreak. But in the desert?

It was no country for ambush. He could see a couple of miles in each direction—could have seen farther if not for shimmery heat waves. The captain began pulling in his skirmishers. When no second wave of attack materialized, he got the train under way again. But this time the *carretas* rolled three abreast, which made a compact unit with less perimeter to defend.

The attackers sulked just beyond range for half an hour, paralleling the *juaristas'* progress along the strip of soft ground. Suddenly Slocum realized what it was. It had changed since the last time he passed through here. Finally the solid citizens rode away. "Do you think they'll be back?" the captain asked.

Slocum shrugged. "I'd fear them not half so much as I would their telegraph. There's still an army detachment at Fort Yuma, is there not?"

The captain nodded soberly.

"And you command a foreign force well within the borders of the United States." Slocum grinned. "Quite apart from all that gold."

"Your army still chases Indians beyond our border all the time," the captain snapped.

"The Army of the United States," Slocum said, correcting him. "And besides, that's different."

"Ah?"

"One must not interfere when the policemen of the world are enforcing their mandate."

The captain gave Slocum a fishy look. "Really believe that, don't you?"

"You believe in Juárez."

They were both shaking their heads when it all started up again. But this time it was not cavalry charging mounted infantry. Crowley and Giraud had worked at their trade long enough to know what they were doing. "For what we are about to receive," Slocum said, "may we be truly thankful, O Lord."

"Amen." The captain gave Slocum a sardonic salute and began shouting orders.

It settled down to a desultory firefight between two more or less evenly matched groups of seasoned soldiers. *Pelones* dug in behind every tiny irregularity in the desert floor and settled down to wait for the occasional incautious head that showed, and the legionnaires did likewise. An hour passed, punctuated by occasional bursts of firing—and back under that unyoked *carreta* Laura screamed unceasingly until finally the *soldaderas* gave up and gagged her. They knew that if the fight continued this way, soldiers' women would soon be busy enough without having to ride herd on a demented *gringa*.

Slocum tried to analyze his feelings. He had ridden with Crowley and Giraud to collect this gold. He had fought off these *juaristas* the first time they had tried to claim it. But that had been before the legionnaire captains had cheerfully undercut each other in desperate bids for Slocum's support. What would they give for his help now?

To hell with them!

And, most especially, to hell with the pusillanimous solid citizens of San Bernardino who had allowed themselves to fall under the thumb of their own creation. Someday the Chinese and the Irish would own the town. And what was wrong with Slocum? Was he turning against his own kind? He wondered how poor old Mr. Sheffield was making out getting his wagon across the deadline these days. It was against everything Slocum had ever stood for, but he had to admit that this *juarista* captain's claim to the gold seemed slightly better than anyone else's. The only better claim would be that of the Indians who had sweated and died digging it for the Jesuits. And whatever had happened to Mojave Joe?

A minié ball—whined overhead, cutting short Slocum's reverie. What was he going to do with Laura? What was he going to do with himself? What was he going to do about those former comrades-in-arms who were shooting at him and at his wife?

The solid citizens reappeared.

Someone had shamed them out of their funk, Slocum supposed. And now they had discovered the limitations of horse against foot. They mustered just beyond range, and Slocum smiled. They were unspanning a wagon, getting ready to push a rolling fortress toward the *juarista* lines. It could, under other circumstances, prove an embarrassment. Slocum unlimbered the buffalo gun. He lay prone, resting the long-barreled piece on the monopod, and squinted through the brass-bound telescope. Suddenly Slocum knew there really was a God after all. One of the men who milled about the wagon was the deputy sheriff who had squeezed a dollar from Mr. Sheffield.

Slocum aimed for nearly a minute, waiting for the scurrying scoundrel to stand still. Finally he did. Slocum killed him.

"*Buen tiro,*" the captain said, congratulating him.

It *was* a pretty good shot. But Slocum saw what else it was. He had started out killing men who had abused the girl he called his wife. Now . . . The Mexicans had a term for what Slocum saw ahead of him. *Capungo* was what they called a creature who would kill for one dollar. He put powder in the buffalo gun, patched a ball properly, and killed the next one for free.

The citizens withdrew another quarter of a mile, except for those who stayed to man the wagon. They began pushing it toward the *juarista* lines.

Slocum ignored the distant wagon and concentrated on the same target as the front-line *pelones,* relaxing as best he could in the forenoon sun and waiting behind his pack for the incautious movement out there that would expose someone to his buffalo gun. It was a half hour before he got another shot, and then he saw sand spurt behind the already-ducking legionnaire.

The captain was walking up and down the lines in plain view, giving an encouraging word here, a whack over some *pelón's* buttocks with the flat of his sword elsewhere. Slocum remembered the times when he had done the same. This kind of waiting fight used up more officers than any bit of hot-blooded action, for it was only by this incessant and foolhardy parading that enlisted men could be made to hold fast and not give in to their own nerves.

The captain stopped beside Slocum.

"Why don't you come down out of the draft for a minute," Slocum said.

The captain shrugged. "You know how it is."

Slocum did. "This will go on till one side runs out of water," he predicted. When the captain did not reply, he knew there was not all that much left in the *carretas*.

The rolling fort had advanced nearly a quarter of a mile, which left it still about half a mile from the *juarista* lines. It moved more slowly as men discovered that they were not horses and that the noonday sun was no place for either species.

Slocum studied the vehicle. Another hundred yards and he would start shooting under it, blowing away kneecaps. Which reminded him of that prissy hotel man who had not cared to tell him where Laura had gone. Slocum imagined some ideal situation in which the hotel clerk would be pushing that wagon, along with the livery-stable men who had overcharged him in San Bernardino. He populated the attacking party with every perpetrator of insult or petty annoyance who had ever soured a day for him. Wouldn't it be lovely to blow them all to hell!

A broad-brimmed Stetson moved out there beyond the *pelones*. None fired at it. Slocum sighted the cross hairs a yard above that hat and waited. A moment later he saw the ramrod where a face should be. No use wasting a round on that one. He turned back to the wagon. Still too far for him to make out legs behind and underneath it. And, by ginger, was it ever getting hot out here in the sun!

He glanced back to where the horses were picketed around unspanned *carretas*. Now that they had gagged her, Laura could no longer scream. Would she suffocate, gagged in this heat? Would that be the solution to his problem in spite of what he had told the captain? Another minié ball whizzed and fluttered overhead like ripping cloth in the instant he heard the shot.

There was sudden shrieking of *soldaderas* back among the *carretas*. Probably one of them had been hit. Taking women along on a campaign had always struck Slocum as a poor way to fight. But women were the only commissary, the only cooks, and the only medical corps that existed for Mexican soldiers. Without his *soldadera* no *pelón* was able to feed himself, much less fight. But Slocum still thought it was one hell of a way to use women. He wondered whatever had happened to his woman of those days. No doubt she had passed into *juarista* hands after Querétaro—like any other spoils of war. Like Laura. Had that bullet— Were they wailing for *la pobre gringa loca?* For an instant he almost went back to see. But there were limits to what a man could do during a battle. Leaving the lines was permitted only those who could show blood.

God, was it ever hot!

XXII

Slocum wondered if anyone ever became acclimatized to the desert. Was he seeing double because of the heat or because of the whack the beefy sheriff had given the back of his head? The men pushing the war wagon were suffering, too. Slocum squinted through the telescope, blinking away the fuzziness. He could see legs and feet beneath the wagon box, but only in short flashes before his vision blurred again.

The poor *soldaderas* were really whooping it up back among the *carretas*. He wondered if one of the children had been hit. The captain passed on his interminable patrol-parade. "Would you care to go back and see if you can quiet them?" he asked.

It was a decent fellow's way of telling Slocum to go see if his wife was all right. Slocum nodded. Like the captain, he strode tall and unbending toward the *carretas*. Bullets stopped whizzing when he and the captain were far enough apart no longer to present a single target. He was nearly back to the picket lines when the racket broke out anew. Then he saw her.

Clad only in a petticoat that covered her from waist to knees, Laura ran blindly from the outspanned *carretas*. She dodged two *soldaderas* and ran through the horse lines, her firm breasts flying.

Slocum cursed. She was running directly toward the enemy.

Slocum felt tears of helpless rage. He had no choices left. He tore loose a picket rope and sprang aboard the nearest horse.

Laura was already halfway across the no-man's-land between *juarista* and Legion lines. Legionnaires raised their heads from hiding to wave and cheer. Some blew kisses. Others shouted "*Vives*" at the streaming-haired half-naked beauty who ran toward them.

The townsmen reacted differently. They began firing at her. Slocum screamed in rage and kicked his mount to hurry it. The tired beast could manage no more than a fast trot.

The townsmen fired again. One of the legionnaires shouted curses and turned to fire toward the war wagon. Slocum slapped his mount, and the mare stumbled in the churned-up dirt of the fault line. He had never imagined a girl could run so fast. What would her bare feet look like after half a mile of searing gravel?

Pelones and legionnaires stood, battle forgotten, as they strained for a better view of the chase. A shot whizzed past Slocum, but it was not from the Legion. Those grizzled veterans were outraged by the shots that came from the townsmen and their wagon.

Laura was within yards of the enemy line.

Slocum cursed the dun mare he rode, cursed the desert and the heat and the gold. He had just caught up to her when he felt a sharp tug at his shirt. He swung down and grabbed a handful of flying hair, then got an arm under her shoulders. As he swung her up across the mare's bare back, he knew the bullet had gone through more than his shirt.

Laura smiled. "John," she said. Her eyes were very bright, but clear. "You came for me!"

There were more shots, and men ran toward them. Laura stared at them in horror, then screamed again. Abruptly she was fighting to break free. Slocum held her with his good arm and guided the mare with his knees. By now the legionnaires had made it clear to the townsmen that they would not tolerate anyone's shooting at Slocum and the girl, and the constant whine of bullets ceased. Slocum rode back through the *juarista* lines.

Soldaderas caught the girl as she fell. She fought them, then realized they were women. When John dismounted, she stared at him in horror. There was a strange yellow light in her eyes.

Slocum stood in the desert heat, wanting to go to her but afraid of driving her still further into madness. He felt dizzy, and swayed. Suddenly he was on the ground, and could not remember falling.

"*¡Ay pobrecito!*" The motherly *soldadera* could not have been over sixteen. She fussed over Slocum, using precious water to clean his wound. Slocum looked at himself through dimming eyes and guessed that his luck had not entirely run out. The open furrow along his ribs stood a chance of healing. . . .

When he woke again, the sun had moved but was still high and blazing hot. He heard no sounds of firing. Slocum looked up to see the *juarista* captain.

"Is it over?" Slocum asked.

"I think it soon shall be. Will you live?"

"If you can call this living."

The captain shrugged. "If you can stand, I will ask you to come with me."

Slocum struggled to his feet. His whole side hurt, and there was a ringing in his ears. "Is this important?"

"Perhaps." The captain led him to a small knoll where they could look out across the lines. He pointed.

The churned-up ground of the fault zone had stopped the citizens' war wagon. It was capable of stopping just about everything now. Slocum stared and rubbed his eyes. Lifting his hand sent a flash of pain through his ribs.

The first time he had passed through here, a few days ago, Slocum had fallen into a trench. This morning the ground had been soft but level. Now it piled into a five-foot-high levee that seemed to be growing even as Slocum watched.

"They'll be moving up close behind that," he predicted.

"But my men will not," the captain said.

Slocum considered a moment and understood. These *pelones* were from the volcano and earthquake region of central Mexico. Fault lines were no mystery to them. But the *pelones* would understand and respect them.

"You have been shooting at our attackers," the captain said. He tried absently to twist points to his mustache and failed again. "And now they have shot at you. It would seem that you are committed to our cause."

"Only until we get out of here."

"Will you help us end this stalemate?"

"I'm just as hot and thirsty as you are." Slocum paused. "But I'm not at my best just now. What'd you have in mind?"

"You can call to them."

"Most people can."

The captain nodded. "But none of my people can call to them in English."

"What do you want me to say?"

The captain worked at the tips of his mustache again, then gave up. "Are you all as free of superstition as our liberals think you are?"

"¿Gringos?"

The captain winced.

"I don't know," Slocum confessed. "I've seen plenty of damn-fool ideas in your country, but I don't fancy you've a monopoly on wasting salt over your shoulder or knocking on wood."

"What would they know of that?" The captain pointed at the earth bulge.

"Damned little, I'd fancy."

"Would they know, for example, that when the ground rises like that, it is only a matter of minutes before—"

Slocum gave a cracked laugh. "You want me to warn them?"

"I was thinking more in terms of threats."

"Oh?"

"My thought was of that Hebrew prophet in the Old Testament who overcame the priests of Baal in calling down lightning."

Slocum was startled. "I thought *catolicos* were not encouraged to read the Bible."

"But I am *juarista, reformista.* I have also read the First Book of Kings."

So had Slocum, but it had been a while.

"Four hundred fifty priests called to Baal for a full day, but there was no sign. Then Elijah alone called down a thunderbolt to light his altar fire."

Slocum remembered now. "But he spent the whole day wetting down the mountaintop. I never understood that until I watched telegraphers piss on their ground wires."

"Elijah called down God's fire," the captain said. "If you wish to call it up, you have about ten minutes."

Slocum laughed. "Good idea, but it'd never work. Those who didn't die laughing would be too busy shooting me. Besides, why bother?"

"I had thought to save some lives. But if you do not care—"

"It is not that I do not care. But I would not be believed."

The captain shrugged.

There was an undercurrent of tension throughout the *juarista* camp as the *soldaderas* rounded up children, made sure everyone was out from under *carretas* or anything else heavy. Up ahead the *pelones* were quietly moving back, pouring just enough fire into the other side to keep them from closing the gap. Slocum felt the ground move. "Wouldn't've been time, anyhow," he muttered.

For as far as he could see in either direction, the ridge of loose dirt was abruptly hidden in dust. There was a grinding, growling noise that reminded him of the gullywhomper that had brought sandy water and killed all those horses. Slocum swayed and had to sit down as the earth beneath him slid sideways in a series of skittering jumps.

People were yelling. Screaming, he supposed. But there was too much noise to hear them. It went on for nearly a minute, and each time he thought it was finally over, the earth would shake again and dust would rise anew along the fault line. He remembered the trench he had fallen into. How many times had it opened and closed in the last minute? How many solid citizens and legionnaires were now being buried alive? Perhaps he ought to have warned them not to sit just behind the peak of the ridge. But if God wished to take Slocum's side in a battle, why refuse the help? Slocum thought God owed him a few.

Finally the earth subsided into tiny quivering tremors. Down by the *carretas* women were busy catching horses that had pulled their picket stakes. A small detachment of *pelones* jogged back to help them. The remainder dug into new positions a safe distance from the fault. Dust settled, and Slocum saw that the ridge was gone. So was the war wagon and all its trigger-happy band. More than half the legionnaires were gone. The remainder were numbed by what they had seen, the sudden disappearance of their comrades. Slocum forced himself to his feet and ignored the twinge in his side. He jerked a thumb at a sergeant. *"Veinte hombres y síganme."*

"A sus ordenes, jefe." The sergeant rounded up his detail of twenty *pelones,* and they stepped out. Before the demoralized remainder of the Legion and those few citizens who had not run or been swallowed up knew what was happening, Slocum's squad had their arms and were marching back inside the *juarista* lines. The soles of Slocum's feet did not stop tingling until he was once more across that patch of spongy ground.

Crowley and Giraud had survived the *temblor.* Now they sat in the shade of Captain Alvarez's *carreta* and eyed Slocum with hatred.

"Traitor," Crowley muttered.

Slocum shook his head. "Not at all. I had never properly enlisted in your cause—and the outfit was certainly disbanded by the sheriff."

"You had no reason to fight against us," Giraud said.

"But I did. Captain Alvarez is my host."

Giraud considered that for a moment, then nodded agreement. "Perhaps I would have done the same. The more important question is, what shall we do now?"

"Your choices are few," Captain Alvarez said. "I cannot simply release you. Not to retain your weapons, for you would certainly follow me to regain the gold."

Neither Giraud nor Crowley had anything to say to that.

"You can't go back to the Cross Seven, either," Slocum said. "I expect we'll all be wanted by whatever passes for authority in San Bernardino. They may not look too hard for us, but anyone who stays around is likely to be hanged."

"What will you do?" Crowley demanded.

"Take Laura a long way from here," Slocum said. "After that—*¿quien sabe?*"

"There is a further alternative for all of you," Alvarez said quietly. "Enlist in my cause. Of course, I shall not trust you with weapons until after I have delivered the gold to my *coronel,* but after that you would be as accepted as any others. More, perhaps. You are experienced soldiers. I make no doubt you will all have the same rank as I within the month."

"Not me," Slocum said. "I've got Laura to look after, and that's no life for her."

"You have truth," Alvarez said. He turned to Crowley and Giraud. "And yourselves?"

They looked at each other, then back to Alvarez. Crowley grinned sourly. "Why not? We've no better offers."

Giraud shrugged. "If one cannot fight for oneself, the cause hardly matters. We know these will be able to pay us. . . ."

"You hardly inspire confidence in your loyalties," Alvarez said.

"Nothing we could say would do that," Giraud said. "And yet, consider this: when has the Legion changed sides? When have legionnaires refused to fight, even when all is hopeless? You will recall Camarón."

Alvarez's eyes narrowed. "I recall. I was there." He looked thoughtful. "Again, you have truth. Will you join us?"

"Yes," Giraud said.

Crowley hesitated, then nodded. *"A sus ordenes, jefe."*

"And those others?" Giraud asked. He waved toward the disconsolate remnant of San Bernardino civilians.

"I cannot bring myself to kill them without provocation," Alvarez said. "Even though it will do my cause no good when they report today's events." He pointed toward the foothills to the west. "There is water ten miles that way. In this heat and without horses it will take them a day to reach it and another two to reach a telegraph. By that time we shall be safely across the border. I will leave them here."

"And me?" Slocum asked.

"I will give you four horses," Alvarez said, "and an hour's start before we release those. Is that sufficient?"

"I reckon it'll have to be."

The mad light in Laura's eyes reminded Slocum of her father. "Maybe it runs in the family," he muttered, then cursed himself for the thought.

She seemed to know him, but she would not speak to him. She would hardly look at him. She wanted to cower back into the *carreta* among the *soldaderas,* but she allowed one of the younger girls to help her mount, and she made no resistance as Slocum took her reins and led her away.

"You may still join us," Captain Alvarez said.

"Thanks. I'll remember that," Slocum answered. He turned to Crowley. "Good luck."

"You, too. You *did* vote to convict me in that court-martial, didn't you?"

"Yes." Slocum hesitated. "Things like honor meant a lot to me then."

"And to me," Crowley said. "*Adiós*. Maybe we'll meet again."

"Maybe." As friends, or looking across gun sights? Slocum wondered. He turned and led Laura westward.

Laura flinched but did not scream whenever Slocum stopped to give the horses water. By evening the mad light was gone; now her eyes were the windows of a vacant house.

The sun went down, and they continued their slow pace westward and upward into the hills. The horses were tiring, but it would be dangerous to stop. The townspeople would be coming, and they would not be friendly toward John Slocum.

One horse in particular seemed to be laboring heavily, and Slocum halted again to inspect the load. He hefted the panniers, and one seemed particularly heavy. "What's the captain given us?" he asked out loud.

Laura didn't answer.

Slocum opened the pannier. It was full of gold.

XXIII

Slocum gave a cracked laugh, which brought a fresh bout of cowering and trembling from Laura. Good God, whatever was he going to do with the poor girl? She seemed almost tractable among women, as long as there was no shooting or cavalry charge to excite her. But she had passed through too many male hands ever to be comfortable within sniffing range of the most docile of men. He could not bring himself to kill her. How could he keep her alive?

He got her back in the saddle and they pushed on, stumbling in the velvety blackness. Toward midnight, if he was reading the Dipper right, a hint of coming moon appeared behind them. Finally they were emerging from the dark of the moon, now that his journey was practically over.

Borrego Springs was populated by a family of Indians who might have been related to Mojave Joe. They fled when Slocum approached, then returned cautiously to beg for things he either did not have or could not afford to give away. They spoke no English. He tried Spanish and met with an equal lack of success.

Laura recovered her voice enough to scream when they came to beg. They stared at her and made signs, knowing her to be mad.

He saw the horses watered and his goatskin filled; then they were on their way once more, climbing more steeply now up out of the desert floor toward those mountains that had cut off yesterday afternoon's sun an hour early. By daylight Slocum's wound was bothering him more than he cared to admit. Face drawn, he forced the stumbling horses up the rock gorge toward the first few scrubby pines. So he was suffering. How about the girl behind him whose hands were lashed to the saddle horn?

He was startled out of his half doze by the sudden swiveling of Dorkus's ears. They were pointing straight ahead. Before Slocum had time to take evasive action he heard clearly the sound that had alerted his horse. Be damned if it wasn't a bell!

A half hour later he was leading his animals into the *placita* before an adobe building. There were Indians here, but these wore trousers and were not as timid as those back at the spring. Slocum tried to remember which order had taken over the missions in California once the Jesuits had been ordered out. Was it the Franciscans or Dominicans? A woman appeared in the doorway. He remembered the *juarista* captain: "Another twenty miles up in the mountains you'll find a Carmelite convent."

"Buenos días, madre," Slocum said.

The square-faced woman returned the greeting. She seemed slightly confused. They came closer to each other, and he saw the nun's eyes were blue. "You do speak English, don't you?" she asked. Slocum suspected she hailed from one of the Rhineland principalities. An idea began to form in his mind. This was an isolated mission, a convent. . . .

"I've a woman here," he began. "My wife has been ill-used by a great many men." Slocum hesitated another moment and saw no reason to lie. "Most of whom are no longer alive."

The *madre superiora*'s face was noncommittal.

"Now she fears all men."

"And you think to leave her where she will see no men?"

Slocum nodded.

The *madre* sighed. "We will do what we can. But you must realize this is a poor order. We grow our own food, make our own clothes."

But I have gold, Slocum thought. Captain Alvarez obviously intended me to use it to care for Laura. The captain's politics might be questionable, but he was a decent man. It had been a while since Slocum had met one. Jesus, how his side was aching.

The *madre* was Palatinate German, but the other nuns were Mexican or Indian. They got Laura off the horse and took her inside where she would not have to endure the expressionless gaze of these slightly built men who struggled to control their fear of madness. Slocum saw to his animals and bedded down in a stable. He wanted to tell the *madre superiora* something, but she was off tending to other duties, and before she returned, Slocum was sound alseep. He did not awaken until the evening bell for the Angelus.

"We will do what we can for her," the *madre* said over a supper of pinole gruel. "Idleness is the worst that can happen in these cases. She will be fed as well as the rest of us, and she will be kept busy at whatever she can learn to do."

"Would a little gold smooth that path for your order?"

"Those who depend on miracles expect too much of a busy God," the *madre* said.

Slocum gave her all of it. There had been enough there to buy a farm, to give himself a fresh start into respectability. Still, he gave her all of it.

Later that night Slocum sat outside the stable where he had bedded down. An Indian had sold him an immense bundle of homemade cheroots for the dime he had found in one pocket. Slocum sat blowing smoke into the night. Even if he could return there, he never wanted to see San Bernardino again. He had excluded himself from *anglo* society in California. He had refused to join the *juaristas*. Who would have him now?

Tiburcio Vásquez? At least that man was an honest bandit who made no pretensions of being anything else. Slocum wondered if he could find him again. If not Vásquez, perhaps he could find Mojave Joe and they could go into the banditry business for themselves. It seemed a growing industry in these parts. He was surprised at how easily he could seriously consider becoming an outlaw. He had come a long way from Virginia Military Academy.

In sudden decision he went into the stable and saddled up, then rode furiously away from the mission. He did not look back.